The Dark Man, By Referral
And Less Pleasant Tales

Chuck McKenzie

www.daftnotions.com

First published by Daft Notions in 2024
Daft Notions www.daftnotions.com
Melbourne, Victoria, Australia
Copyright © Chuck McKenzie

National Library of Australia Cataloguing-in-Publication data.
The Dark Man, By Referral and Less Pleasant Tales
ISBN: 978-0-6458945-2-3 (paperback)
ISBN: 978-0-6458945-3-0 (ebook)

Spelling in this collection is standard Australian

Cover Design and Interior Artwork by Greg Chapman
Editing © All In The Edit www.allintheedit.com

Fiction, Horror, Short Stories

About the Author

Chuck McKenzie was born in 1970 and is still not dead. He is an award-nominated author of numerous science fiction and horror stories, and he hopes one day to be described by his neighbours as having seemed like such a nice man. You can stalk him on Instagram at **@chuck.mckenzie.author**

Also by Chuck McKenzie

Worlds Apart (Novel, Hybrid Publishers 1999)

AustrAlien Absurdities: Comic Tales of Science-Fiction, Fantasy & Horror by Australian Authors (Anthology, Co-edited with Tansy Rayner-Roberts, Agog! Press 2001)

Confessions of a Pod Person (Collection, MirrorDanse Editions 2005)

Conversations With My Cat (Co-authored with MacReady McKenzie and Ripley McKenzie, Daft Notions 2023)

Dedication

To Mum and Dad, who always supported me in everything I ever did. I miss you both terribly.

To those who supported and encouraged me at the very beginning of my writing career—Bill Congreve, Cat Sparks, Robert Hood, Sarah Endacott, KM Stevenson, and others—as well as those whose enthusiasm and gentle prodding lured me back to writing after so many years away from the field—Lindy Cameron, Katya de Beccara, Narrelle M. Harris, and everyone else who provided encouragement and validation.

To my kids, neither of whom remember my first cycle of churning out fiction, but seem vaguely pleased and intrigued by my return to it.

And to Sarah, who holds my heart every single day. (Have you considered putting it in a jar, Sweetie? It'd make less of a mess…)

Contents

The Dark Man, By Referral

The small cardboard sign pinned to the tray read *'Orrible 'Airy Spiders–$1 Each* in spooky lettering, and James kept his eyes on it; partly because he found the obvious misspellings thrilling in a way he couldn't have put into words, and partly (mostly) because it meant he could sort of keep an eye on the Dark Man without looking at his face, and James didn't want to get a good look at that face, because he felt that if he did he would lose his mind. James thought about all the times Trent had yelled that the Dark Man would come for him for being a little shit, which to James—up until a few moments ago—had been a far less frightening thought than the prospect of what Trent might do to him. Now, though, he stood gripped by a fear so all-consuming that he couldn't even summon up the ability to run the dozen or so steps that would take him from the deepening dusk to the (relative) safety of home; so instead, because it was all he could seem to do, he focussed upon the sign and upon not looking at the Dark Man's face.

The brief glimpse James had caught of that face, as he'd turned from waving goodnight to Tim and impossibly found the legendary monster of Stanhope standing before him in the street, had given him a sense of *wrongness* that went beyond fear; it was the same feeling he'd often felt when watching Dad's favourite old horror movies on

Saturday nights, but now inducing nausea instead of thrills without Dad there to cuddle him.

"Master James Kent?" the Dark Man asked.

James blinked, automatically looked up from the sign ("*Look at me when I'm talking to you, ya little shit!*") and cringed in expectation of awfulness, before realising he could hardly even see the Dark Man's face, hidden in shadow thrown by the black, wide-brimmed hat the Dark Man wore. And the Dark Man's clothes…well, he looked like he was wearing one of those robes that nuns wore, and the thought almost made James giggle. Then his thoughts turned back to his immediate situation, and the urge to giggle died. Even standing a few metres away, the Dark Man seemed to tower in a way that adults only did when they were up close and about to hurt you.

James opened his mouth but found himself unable to utter a word.

"I do apologise if I've alarmed you, Master James. That certainly wasn't my intention." The Dark Man's voice was deep and rich, and immediately made James think of Christopher Lee in the Dracula movies.

"How…do you know my name?" James managed.

"I know your name, Master James, because I have in fact been *referred* to you." The Dark Man paused. "Do you know what *referred* means?"

James shook his head. He thought maybe it meant something medical, as he'd heard his GP use the word before.

"Well, it means that someone who has found my services useful has specifically suggested I approach you, because they feel that you, also, might value my services. In other words, they *referred* me to you."

James stared into the shadows covering the Dark Man's face, feeling it looked too *still* in there when the Dark Man spoke. "Who…*referred* me?" he asked, rolling the word around his mouth.

"Ah, now, that would be Master Timothy Brown, at number forty-two."

James automatically turned his head to look down the street, half-expecting to see Tim standing there. All he saw was the sun beginning to slip below the horizon, and with that came the thought of being caught out in complete darkness alone with the Dark Man. James hurriedly turned back, to find the Dark Man had silently closed the gap between them and was now definitely within grabbing distance, arms outstretched. James stumbled back a pace. But the Dark Man stood motionless, black-gloved hands holding out the tray to James. It was one of those wooden trays that James sometimes saw old men in suits holding when he went to the railway station with Mum. Instead of poppies and pins, though, this tray was filled with…well, James guessed they were the 'Orrible 'Airy Spiders mentioned on the sign; a mass of whitish-grey egg-shaped objects, each with multiple long, furry-looking legs extending in all directions, and dozens of tiny red eyes clustered around a weird, puckered orifice. No fangs or spinnerets, so not very much like Spiders at all, thought James. They glistened like rotten peaches and jiggled slightly, even though the Dark Man was standing perfectly still.

"Why do they look all sticky?"

"Because they *are* sticky. One throws them against a wall, and the stickiness allows them to walk down that wall."

James had seen sticky toys that worked the same way before, though he'd never owned one. And suddenly, despite the gross look of the things—or maybe even because of it—he really wanted one.

"Would you like one?" the Dark Man asked, as though reading James' thoughts.

James instinctively reached out towards the tray, then hesitated. "I don't have any money," he admitted. "And I'm not supposed to take stuff from strangers."

The hat dipped in acknowledgement. "A sensible policy. Master Timothy calls me Mister Black, as does Mistress Heather Noake on the corner, whom I believe you also know, and several other Masters and Mistresses hereabouts."

"Okay."

"You see, Master James, the wonderful thing about referrals is that the person referring me to another already knows and trusts me, just as they know and trust you, so you needn't worry about me despite me being a stranger."

James began to nod, then suddenly remembered a scene from one of Dad's movies where a clown in a drain introduces himself to a little boy and tells the boy that the two of them are no longer strangers, and then… But the clown in that movie hadn't been *referred*. And how would the Dark Man—Mister Black—know everyone's names if they didn't already know *him?* And anyway, Mister Black could already have grabbed James a dozen times over if he'd wanted to, so…

"Okay," James said again. "Yeah. That makes sense, I guess."

"As to the cost," and here, Mister Black pushed the tray a little closer to James, "there is none."

"It says a dollar on the sign."

"That sign," Mister Black said, "is for adults, who would not understand that some do not require money for their services."

James nodded, not really understanding. He reached out and gingerly pulled one of the Spiders from the top of the tray. It quivered in his hand, sticking lightly to his skin, cool and feeling like a half-set jelly. The red eyes stared blindly up at him. "Thank you," he said, remembering his manners.

"You are very welcome," Mister Black intoned, withdrawing the tray. "I hope you will enjoy it. Oh. And, ah," he added, as James began to turn away. "Should you find at any point that you no longer require the Spider, all you need do is simply bring it out to the street, and I shall collect it."

"Okay," said James, thinking how unlikely it was that he'd want to return a toy. "But how will you know to be here if I do?"

"I'll know," said Mister Black. And he stood and watched as James turned and raced the darkness home.

James lay face-up and wrong-way-around on his bed, flinging the Spider at the wall as though it were a tennis ball. At first, he tried throwing as hard as he could, but found that the mattress prevented him from pulling his arm back sufficiently to aim properly. The Spider ended up splatting just above the bedhead then dropping a centimetre or two before hitting the wooden frame, whereupon it would simply peel off the wall and drop behind the pillows, forcing James to sit up and rummage for it. After a few such attempts he changed tactic and tried lobbing the Spider like a shot-put, placing it in his palm then pulling his arm back flat against the mattress next to his head before 'releasing' like one of those giant Roman catapults. The Spider flew in a graceful arc, hitting the top of the wall, and stuck there for a moment, shuddering. James allowed himself a small, muted cheer. The Spider began a slow roll down the wall, rubbery legs shooting out to slap against the plaster then detaching as they were drawn in under the egg-shaped body, only to spray out again in a shower of grasping limbs as the body completed each roll. It took about ten seconds for the Spider to hit the bedhead this time, whereupon it bounced off the top and dropped onto the pillow below, then rolled down and came to rest against the soles of James' feet.

Cool.

James sat up and retrieved the Spider, before resuming his catapulting position. On the second try, the Spider rolled past his foot and ended up just short of James' outstretched hand. That seemed odd. The bed was perfectly flat, and he wouldn't have thought the sticky toy could roll half the length of the mattress. He craned his neck and regarded the Spider warily. The Spider seemed to stare back at him, red eyes glistening. James hesitated, then stretched out his hand, retrieved the Spider, and tried another throw. This time, the Spider rolled all the way into James' outstretched hand, jiggling against his palm. James held the Spider up to his face, not entirely sure what it was he was looking for.

On the next throw, the Spider hit the wall and dropped straight down behind the pillows again.

James sat up and scrambled to retrieve the toy, noting that the Spider was now coated with a thin layer of dust that presumably counteracted the stickiness. James rubbed at the dust, then licked his finger and tried again, with no success. Annoyed, he rolled off his bed and left his room.

Mum was in the kitchen, cutting vegetables. The muffled sound of the telly told James that Trent was in the living room.

"Mum?"

"What's up, buddy?" Mum favoured him with a bright smile.

"How do you clean sticky toys?"

"Sticky toys?" Mum spotted the Spider in James' hand. "Ah, wall-walkers. Umm…warm soapy water, I think."

"Won't that wash the sticky stuff off it?

"I don't think so. In fact, I think it sort of revitalises it?"

"How?"

"Not sure. Heard it somewhere. Want me to Google it?"

"Google what?" asked Trent from the kitchen doorway, and James' heart shrank.

"Cleaning one of those wall-walkers," Mum said, too brightly. "One of those things you throw against the wall, and it sort of crawls down."

"Yeah, I know what a wall-walker is. I'm not fuggin' stupid."

Mum's smile vanished, and her eyes briefly met James'. *Don't poke the bear*. Trent's tone had been lightly mocking, but that could easily escalate.

"Ay, Jimmy. Show us."

James slowly turned, keeping his upturned palm close to his body.

Trent sniffed, ran the back of his hand across his nose, and slouched into the kitchen. Came in close (*too close*) to James, towering over him, looking down at the Spider with a sneering half-smile on his face. "Where'd ya get it?"

"A…friend gave it to me."

Trent snorted. He looked up to smirk at Mum, then turned back to James, darkness clouding his features. The loosened tie hanging beneath five-o-clock jowls made Trent look a bit like a mean Homer Simpson, thought James. "Steal it, didya?"

"No!" There was a time when Mum would have immediately jumped in to defend James, but James knew Mum had learned the hard way to not do that. The faint scar across his cheek prickled in anticipation.

"Who gave it to ya, then?"

"Tim." James met Trent's gaze and held it.

Trent stared, then gave Mum a querying look.

"James' friend from up the road."

Trent looked back at James. "And Timmy'll back that up, will he?"

James suddenly felt confident that Tim would do exactly that. It occurred to him that neither he nor any of the other kids would want to tell an adult about Mister Black. It was a shared secret, like a sort of club, and the notion gave him a thrill. "Yep," he said.

Trent eyed him coldly, then sniffed again. "Better not be lying, or there'll be *consequences*. The Dark Man doesn't like kids who lie."

James only just managed to hold back an hysterical giggle.

"Dinner?" Trent asked, not breaking eye-contact with James.

"Ten minutes. Just gotta boil—"

"Fine." Trent turned and slouched back out of the kitchen. A few seconds later, the volume of the telly increased.

James heard Mum exhale quietly and turned to find she'd already gone back to preparing dinner. *Why do you let him stay here, Mum?* But there was no point asking the same old question. Once, Mum would have said it was because she was lonely. But James knew that was no longer the reason.

Sometimes he wished Trent was just…gone. He couldn't quite bring himself to wish anything worse. Not after Dad's accident.

"Mum?"

"Mm?"

"Do you think the Dark Man is real?"

Mum turned, her gaze flickering momentarily to the kitchen doorway. She took a couple of steps closer to James and, lowering her voice, said: "Do *you* think the Dark Man's real?"

James took a moment to consider how best to answer, then simply shrugged. It seemed the safest response.

Mum nodded. "Okay then. Well, no, he's not real. At least, not the Dark Man Trent talks about." Seeing James' blank look, she sighed. "Monsters aren't real, buddy. What happened was…there was a sickness that made a lot of locals really ill, and some of them died, and

I think people just made up this story about a Dark Man to sort of…help them cope with it. Sometimes it's easier to blame a person, or even a made-up monster, than it is to blame a random disease."

"Why?"

"Dunno. It's just something people do. And this all happened decades ago, long enough for the Dark Man to pass into local legend."

James digested that. "So…Dad grew up in Stanhope. Was he here when all this happened?"

"Yeah, he was. Trent, too."

James frowned. "Dad loved horror stuff, but he never told me anything about the Dark Man, or the sickness, or anything like that."

Mum hesitated. "Sometimes real life is scarier than horror. The disease affected people that Dad knew, and I think maybe he just didn't want to remember. He never told me much about it either, even after I moved here to be with him. And he probably didn't want to talk about the Dark Man, because the legend's now so closely linked to the true story. Does that make sense?"

"I guess. Did Trent know people who got sick? Or died?"

"Probably, yeah."

"So why does *he* always talk about the Dark Man?"

"Trent…just wants you to behave." The pain of the lie was obvious on Mum's face. "If someone told you the Dark Man would get you if you didn't wash your hands after you went to the toilet, you'd wash your hands, wouldn't you? And then you hopefully wouldn't have any disease on your hands. So really those sort of legends are meant to keep you safe."

James gave Mum a look.

"Okay, so sometimes people just make up stuff to get kids to behave. Remember when you used to believe in Santa, and you'd behave so Santa would bring you toys?"

"I was eight. I'm twelve now."

Mum smiled sadly. "Yeah. Just about ready to move out and get a job."

James snorted.

"Okay, enough talk about scary stuff," Mum said. "Go wash up, buddy." She nodded towards the Spider. "And give that thing a wash too, if you like."

James nodded and turned towards the kitchen door.

"James?"

James turned back.

"Don't use any of what we've discussed as an excuse to—"

"I won't!" James said, emphatically.

"And maybe just don't mention this talk at all, okay?"

James nodded.

"Good boy."

Mum and James were already eating dinner, one of the few discourtesies Trent would allow (except for those occasions when he didn't), when the swearing began out in the hall. They froze, forks half-raised to their mouths.

"The fugg is this??" Trent thundered, striding into the kitchen. James cringed as Trent thrust out his fist, rubbery grey legs dangling between his fingers.

Mum swallowed her food, looking ill. "That's just James' toy—"

"*I know what it is!*" Trent rounded on her, and she shrank into herself. "Ya think I'm fuggin' *retarded*??" He swung back to glare at James, looking like a dog about to attack. "What's it doing in the fuggin' bathroom?" A beat. "*Eh??*"

"I had to wash it," James croaked. He wished Mum would say something, defend him, even if it meant that Trent's rage focussed upon her instead. His cheek prickled.

"THEN YOU WASH IT OUTSIDE!!"

Mum made a small noise. Trent swung back to her, leaning over her, pushing his face into hers. "WHAT??"

Mum licked her lips. "I just…Trent, where's the harm?"

An expression of rabid incredulity crossed Trent's face. "Leavin' his shit all over the fuggin' place? It's not his fuggin' HOUSE!!"

James suddenly found himself filled with utter rage. *It's not yours either! It's mine and Mum's and Dad's and one day I'll be big enough to throw you out if Mum won't do it!*

Something of what he was thinking must have shown on his face. Trent looked at him, and his expression went blank. Then he smiled.

Oh shit, thought James.

Trent straightened up and casually strolled over to James, then squatted down on his haunches so their faces were level. "Whaddaya thinking, Jimmy?" he asked quietly. "Maybe you wanna have a go, eh?"

I'd like to punch you so hard you cry.

"Yeah? Wanna take a swing?"

The silence seemed to stretch forever.

"Yeah, that's what I thought."

Trent started to straighten, then abruptly thrust his face back towards James with a grunt. A fake-out attack. James had known it was coming, but still couldn't stop himself from flinching, and was immediately filled with self-loathing. Trent gave a short, ugly bark of laughter. "Fugg with me, and there'll be fuggin' *consequences*." He spun on his heel and flung the Spider hard through the kitchen doorway. A soft thud sounded from the hallway beyond. Trent grabbed his plate, gave James and Mum a hard stare, then loped back to the loungeroom to eat in front of the telly.

After a long silence, Mum reached over and touched James' hand. "Hang in there, buddy," she murmured. "Things'll get better."

James pulled his hand away and went back to eating his dinner, carefully regarding the plate in front of him. Only once did he look up, to find Mum staring miserably at him. The shame in her eyes made him feel so bad that he went back to staring at his plate again.

After talking about all the usual stuff—school, mutual friends, girls, and so on—James asked Tim the question he really wanted an answer to: "Why did you refer Mister Black to me?"

Tim dropped his gaze to the road. "Remember when you came to school with stitches across your cheek?" He glanced up at James. "And you told us all you'd run full speed into a door frame?"

James flushed, hoping Tim couldn't see it in the gloom.

Tim nodded. "Yeah. Well. Last school holidays I got some really bad bruising, here." He clamped his right hand tightly around his left wrist for a moment. "Healed up before school started again. There were other times, though…" He gave James a hard look. "Heather referred Mister Black to me. And I haven't had any more bruising since."

James couldn't quite get a fix on what Tim was saying, and couldn't think of the right questions to ask, and the look Tim was giving him was beginning to make him squirm.

"Don't worry," Tim said, eventually. "It'll all make sense."

"*What* will?" James asked in frustration. "I don't understand!"

"You will. I promise. And then things'll be better."

"My mum always says that," James blurted, sourly.

"Mine too. And now things *are* better. You'll see."

James shook his head in exasperation, then noticed how dark it had gotten. "I better get going. Trent's in a shitty mood today. I'm surprised he's not out here yelling for me to come in."

"Yeah, my dad used to do that," Tim said. He smiled, and the interplay of shadow and light from the nearest lamppost seemed to stretch the smile into a maniacal Joker's grin. "But he's sick at the moment. *Really* sick. So." Tim shrugged. "Later." He turned and ambled away into the darkness.

"Has your dad got Covid?" James called after him. But Tim didn't reply.

Trent was already snoring in front of the telly when James got back inside. James spent a few minutes unsuccessfully searching the hallway for the Spider, before sadly concluding that Trent had disposed of it. James said goodnight to Mum, sitting at her work laptop in the kitchen, then went to bed and glared at the ceiling until he finally fell asleep.

"Late shift today?" Mum asked, hesitantly.

Trent slumped into his seat with a groan. "Not going. Already rung in."

"How come?"

"Feel like shit."

James risked a quick glance up from his cornflakes. Trent had dark smudges under his eyes, contrasted by a pallid, sweaty face.

Mum gave Trent a worried look. "Yeah. You don't look great. Maybe a bit of breakfast?"

Trent grunted. "No breakfast. Gonna sleep it off."

"Okay. But maybe go to bed, yeah? You might have cricked your neck last night on the couch."

"Nah, I'll stick with the couch." Trent gave Mum a bleary look, daring her to push the point. She didn't.

So, Trent had spent the night in the loungeroom. It suddenly occurred to James that his Spider might be in there also. Maybe it had bounced off the hallway wall. And if so, Trent obviously hadn't found it or they'd be hearing all about it right now. James eyed the kitchen doorway, weighing his chances of checking out the loungeroom before Mum had to drive him to school on her way to work.

"Should you go and get a Covid test?" Mum asked. "A few people in the street have been getting sick. They had to take Glen Brown to hospital, though Jane says it's not Covid. God, that's all we need, another outbreak, probably a lockdown—"

"Fuggsake, it's just 'flu!" Trent snapped, though with less force than James would have expected.

"Okay then. Well, stay warm and drink plenty of water. James? All set? Need to be in the car in five, buddy."

"But—" *But you're not supposed to go to work or school if you've been around someone with Covid. You have to get a test, and then wait at home until—*

Mum stared at James. Her eyes flicked to the back of Trent's head, then back to James.

Home all day with Trent.

"Just…need to get my pencil case," James mumbled, through a final mouthful of cereal.

Mum glanced at James' schoolbag, sitting on the floor beside his chair. "Okay. Go on, then."

James got up, moved carefully past Trent, and went down the hallway towards his room. Then he quietly doubled back and slipped into the loungeroom. He scanned the floor, then dropped to his hands and knees and peered underneath the couch. Nothing. Then, despite knowing it was an utterly ridiculous place to look, James leaned over the back of the couch, and pulled aside the cushions.

And there it was. Looking up at him, quivering.

James snatched up the Spider and examined it quickly. All in one piece. No legs torn off. Indeed, the Spider looked *healthier* than when James had seen it last, the colour having changed from sickly grey-white to a pinkish-grey. Maybe that was just something it did. James was sure he'd heard of toys that did that.

The grating of chair legs on linoleum jolted him back to the moment. Instinctively he stuffed the Spider back behind the cushions, then scuttled out into the hallway. A half-second later, Trent loomed in the kitchen doorway. "Whaddya doing? Where's your pencil case?"

"I think it's in my bag after all." No reaction. "I thought I hadn't packed it, but I think I just need to have a better look."

Trent eyed him for a moment, then grunted and shuffled his way past James and vanished into the loungeroom. James went into the kitchen, where Mum was jingling the car keys. "I heard that. In your bag after all, you reckon?" She smiled and unzipped his school bag, revealing the pencil case sitting on top of his books and lunch box.

"Well, whaddya know?" Mum leaned towards James and stage-whispered: "You must've had a Man's Look the first time, eh?" The tone was jovial, but the look in her eye told James her 'bullshit detector' was pinging.

He lowered his gaze. "Yeah."

"Well, that's okay. Got everything now? Let's go." She didn't call out to Trent as they left.

The house was silent when they got home that afternoon. After looking in on Trent, asleep in the loungeroom, Mum busied herself rifling through the fridge for the makings of dinner, while James hesitated at the hallway door. From the darkness beyond he could hear the familiar rasp of Trent's snoring. Mum stopped moving around behind him, and James could feel her eyes on the back of his head. "Go on, then," she urged. "Homework?"

"A little bit."

"Okay, homework first, then you can go outside for a bit while it's still light. Quietly, though."

As soon as he got to his room, James fished his school laptop out of his bag, opened it up on his desk and began Googling. There were a few mentions of the Dark Man as a local legend; a black-clad monster who preyed upon naughty children. There were maybe a dozen links to articles about the 'Stanhope Outbreak' of 1989, all of which mentioned a 'wasting disease' that affected ninety-three people, twenty-seven of whom had died. All adults. No kids. And there was one article mentioning that Stanhope actually had a long history of unexplained outbreaks going back almost 150 years and occurring at intervals of a few decades, the 1989 outbreak being the most recent. At the end of that article the journalist suggested that the legend of the Dark Man was likely to have started with the founding of the town in 1857, as it seemed a rather 'old fashioned' tale.

Um...Slenderman? The Blair Witch? Then James saw the article was from 1993.

And that was it. Nothing more. Although maybe the site blocker on the laptop was filtering out anything more gory or creepy.

And then James remembered the Spider.

Creeping down the hallway, James paused at the open door to the lounge room, peering into the gloom beyond. The blinds were down, thin rays of daylight filtering in at the bottom in a way that made the darkness inside seem like it was made of brown dust. James strained his eyes as shapes in the darkness began to resolve themselves, and he took a step in the direction of the couch.

A floorboard creaked under his foot, and he froze.

The snoring stopped. Something rolled sluggishly in the dark. A groan. Some muttered gibberish. Then a sudden cessation of movement and sound.

James took a step back.

"Wha're you doing?" Trent's voice was slow and slurred.

James froze for a moment, then licked his lips. "We're home."

A beat. "You're home." It wasn't a question. It didn't even sound like Trent's usual trick of repeating something you'd said to make you feel stupid for saying it. It was more like Trent was trying to get his head around the words, repeating them simply to get a feel of the meaning. Like his head wasn't in the right space.

A strange feeling overcame James; a sudden thrill he'd never before experienced outside of the school playground. The sensing of weakness in another. An immediate desire to push and see what happened, regardless of *consequences*. He hesitated.

Then—

"That's what I said. We're home," he said, not quite adopting the level of contempt that Trent would have under the same circumstances.

Silence.

"What?" The word came crisp and clear, without slurring.

Oh shit.

"WHAT??" Trent bellowed, and James suffered a moment of utter regret, frozen to the spot, before Trent reared up out of the darkness like a malevolent jack-in-the-box, jumping up from the couch. "YOU WATCH YOUR FUGGIN'—!"

And then he stopped and seemed to fold in upon himself without actually collapsing, tilting forwards, arms flopping down by his sides, mouth dropping open. He looked, thought James, like the flapping inflated figure at the place where Mum got the car serviced, but with the air gushing out of it, and that was somehow even more alarming than the threat of Trent's violence.

Something bulbous and gelid fell from Trent's neck, hitting the floor with a soft thud and rolling under the couch.

"MUM!" James yelled, and instantly Mum was there. *She must've been standing outside the loungeroom since Trent started yelling,* thought James, *but she only came in when I yelled too. Was she waiting until he started hitting me?*

Trent staggered, clutched at the side of the couch, and half-sat, half-fell on to the armrest, gasping like a beached fish, his face so pale that the dim light from the hallway seemed to make it glow. Mum pushed past James, rushing to Trent's side. "What's wrong??" Trent goggled at her, shakily raising a hand to press his fingers into the soft flesh of his neck. Mum pushed his fingers aside. James leaned forwards, expecting to see bruising, blood, bite-marks. Nothing but sweat and stubble. Mum peered into Trent's face. "Trent? Trent! Can you breathe?" No response. Mum gave a huff of panic and irritation. "Come on, come out to the kitchen…" She bent and heaved one of Trent's arms up over her shoulder, wrangling him into a standing position, then shuffled both of them out of the loungeroom.

James hesitated, then knelt down on the carpet and stuck his hand under the couch. His fingers closed around the Spider almost immediately, and he withdrew his arm to examine it. The thing quivered (or throbbed?) against his palm—surely *bigger* than the last time he'd seen it. And it felt warm. Hot, even. And even in the gloom, James could see the Spider's pink tinge had deepened almost to crimson.

James had the sudden impression of a creature that had just enjoyed a hearty meal.

"James!"

James bounced to his feet, thrust the Spider into his pocket, and ran to the kitchen.

Mum had Trent sitting at the table. "Did you see what happened?" she asked, as James entered. "He keeps touching his neck, but there's no injury, and I think he's breathing okay, but—Trent? Shall I call an ambulance?" Trent shook his head emphatically, and made as if to get up, groaning weakly.

Mum placed a hand against his chest. "No, stop, you need to—"

Trent glared at her. Mum's face blanched as Trent slowly reached up to grasp the offending hand, his fingers scrabbling for purchase, seeking out the familiar weak spots, the holds where fingers could be crushed together.

Eventually, without any obvious effort, Mum pulled her hand free, placed it upon Trent's own, and pushed it down against the table. Then held it there. Trent grunted, the muscles in his arm flexing ineffectually.

An expression crept over Mum's face that James had never seen there before.

James shuffled awkwardly. Mum looked at him. "Hey, buddy. How about you go to your room for a bit? I'm going to give the hospital a call, okay?"

James nodded and went to his room, lying on his bed and holding the Spider, listening to Mum talk on the phone, her voice high and urgent at first, slowly lowering in pitch as the call continued. Then a second, far more restrained call. Then the sounds of Mum helping Trent to the bedroom. Eventually Mum appeared in the doorway to James' room. "We can't get Trent into hospital just yet. The local ones are all full of Covid patients."

"Okay," said James, and then, because he felt like maybe it was the question Mum would expect him to ask: "Does Trent have Covid?"

"The ambos said it didn't sound like it, but whatever he's got still seems pretty bad. I'll duck out soon and pick up some tests for all of us. In the meantime, maybe just stay in your room. Tim's mum says there's a few people in the street with something similar, so…y'know."

"Kids?"

Mum shook her head. "Parents. But you'd hate to be the first kid with it, eh?"

"Sure."

Mum smiled and nodded. "Just let me know if you need anything before I pop out."

"Can I go out and talk to Tim?" James nodded towards the darkening window. "He's usually out there around now."

"Well…I mean, not if there's a chance Trent has Covid." Mum lowered her eyes. "You and I shouldn't even have gone to school and work today, really, except—"

"What if I just talk to him from the driveway?"

Mum mulled it over for a second. "Okay, sure. But keep your distance, okay?"

"It was attached to his *neck*."

Tim nodded. "How's it looking?"

"What do you mean?"

"Like, is it looking…well-fed?"

"Yeah," James said, slowly. "It is."

"Cool. And how's Trent looking?"

James shrugged. "Not great."

"And…how do you feel about that?"

James considered. "Fine."

Tim nodded again. "Can I give you some advice? When he's sleeping, try to make sure the Spider's always in the room with him. It'll move things along quicker."

"I will. Thanks," James said.

"You're welcome," Tim replied.

After he got back inside, James lay on his bed until Mum went out to get the Covid tests. Then he took the Spider, opened the door to Mum's room, stood listening to Trent's gurgling snores for a moment, then gently tossed the Spider into the darkness underarm and closed the door again. Then he went to the loungeroom and watched all the cartoons that Trent never let him watch anymore.

The tests came back negative for all three of them. Regardless, Trent couldn't even talk the next day. Mum called her work and Trent's and the school to say they'd all be off for the next day or so, then left James at home for several hours while she dragged Trent to the GP. James went into Mum's room and found the Spider, swollen, red and pulsing, beneath Trent's sweat-stained pillow. He took it to the bathroom and cleaned the accumulated muck off it, then took the Spider to the loungeroom. He sat it on the couch beside him, making sure its eyes were facing the right way, and they watched telly together. The daytime kids' shows were a bit too childish now for James, but he found them comforting. At some point he began talking to the Spider. Asking questions. *What are you? Are you alive, or part of Mister Black, or something else entirely? How are you making Trent sick?* The Spider remained silent, so eventually James switched to just talking about Stuff. About Dad, and how life had been before, and how much James missed him every day, and how Mum still cried sometimes when Trent wasn't home and she thought James wasn't watching, about Trent, and the things he did, and what James wished would happen to Trent. And he cried a bit, and then a lot, and afterwards felt better than he'd felt in a very long time. And when he heard Mum's car pull into the driveway, he returned the Spider to Mum's room—stowing it back beneath Trent's pillow—and went and lay on his bed and pretended to read a book.

After much huffing and puffing as she put Trent to bed again, Mum came to James' doorway. "Hey, buddy. All good?"

James gave her the thumbs up.

Mum smiled tiredly. "Sorry we took so long. The GP sent us straight on to hospital to get a diagnosis, but they couldn't tell us what Trent's got either, and they still don't have room to admit him for treatment. Just keep on keeping your distance from him, okay?"

"No problem. When do I go back to school?"

"Not for another few days. Whatever this thing is that Trent's got, it's nasty, and we don't want to go spreading it."

"Can we do something if we don't get sick?"

Mum gave James a funny look. "Like what?"

"Maybe the zoo? It's been ages. If Trent's still sick, he doesn't need to come with us." He turned back to his book and pretended not to see the way Mum stared at him, until she finally left.

That night, Mum slept on the couch so as to distance herself from Trent. James briefly considered sneaking into Mum's room to check on the Spider but figured that Trent wasn't likely to tidy the bedclothes, so the Spider would probably stay safely hidden. Cosied up to Trent.

James drifted off to sleep with a small smile on his lips.

The next day Trent couldn't even get out of bed. Mum and James sat quietly in the loungeroom for a while, reading. Eventually Mum sighed, then gave James a look; the sort of look she'd not given him since Trent had come into their lives. The sort of look that hinted at impending fun.

"How about I plug in the PlayStation?"

"What?"

Mum grinned impishly. "No? Worried I'll whip your butt?"

And Mum had pulled the PS4 out of the cupboard, the box grimy with dust and fluff, and the two of them had set it up and played Spider-Man for the rest of the day. It was only when his belly began to rumble that James realised it must be way past dinnertime. And at that thought, he stiffened.

"What's wrong?" Mum asked. And then her eyes widened. She stared at the window, taking in the darkness beyond, then scrambled to her feet and rushed out of the room.

James waited, his guts tightening. Waited for the outrage over dinner being late.

A few moments later Mum came back into the loungeroom. "Trent's not hungry," she said, then paused. "I didn't get anything ready for dinner, so…maybe takeaway? We could get McDonald's…"

And they did.

The day after that they all stayed home again.

It was a good day.

Trent stayed in bed, silent and unmoving.

James and Mum played Monster Hunter all day, with pizza for lunch, eaten on the couch. Dinner was home-made hamburgers with oven-baked chips.

Afterwards, James went outside and talked to Tim from a socially responsible distance. They talked about all the cool movies being put on hold because of the pandemic. They talked about school, and girls. They talked about sports, and the latest electronic games. They talked about cars. And comics. And then, finally:

"My dad's being admitted to a care facility," Tim said. "He can't do anything for himself anymore. Can't get out of bed. Can't feed himself. Can't even wipe his own arse. Doctor says it's some sort of wasting disease. Might be a long-term thing."

"Huh," James said. "And…how do you feel about that?"

Tim's teeth glowed in the lamplight. "Fine."

James nodded. "I Googled the Dark Man."

"Yeah. I think we all do."

"There's hardly anything there."

Tim was silent for a moment, then said: "I think the outbreaks have been small enough that they don't really rate much attention outside of Stanhope. This one won't flag any attention at all, I reckon—not with Covid going on everywhere. And there wouldn't be many adults still in Stanhope who know what's *really* going on—adults who were kids back in nineteen eighty-nine, I mean. The ones who got *referred*. I reckon most of them moved away. Maybe they forgot. Or wrote him off as an imaginary friend they had a kid."

James nodded. "Yeah. And if there *are* any who knew, and stayed, and remembered…I think they'd try really hard to not grow up to be like the adults who got sick."

"Yeah."

They stood for a while, looking at the sunset.

"Feels like we should…pinkie-swear, or something," James said eventually. "Y'know. Secrets. Vow to never become arseholes. That sort of thing."

"Dude!" Tim said, sternly. "I'm not touching you. There's still a Covid pandemic on!"

They laughed at that for far longer than seemed reasonable.

"Trent."

Trent squirmed and blinked against the sudden glare of the bedroom light. He made a soft wheezing sound, then locked eyes with James, standing at the bedside. The confusion on his face slowly morphed to anger. He wheezed again, and the muscles in his neck tightened like knotted rope as he attempted to sit up.

After a moment he stopped and lay trembling, glaring weakly at James.

"You're going to have to be nice to us now, Trent," James said. "To me and Mum. I don't think you'll ever be well enough again to hurt us, but if you don't act nice… Well, I think that's why some of the adults died back in nineteen eighty-nine. Maybe some of the people who got sick were so awful that they ended up with pillows over their faces."

Trent's eyes widened, his gaze flickering to the door behind James.

James leaned in over Trent. "Mum just went to the toilet. We've got a couple of minutes to chat. Anyway, even if you do get well enough to talk properly again, to tell Mum about this, you'd better not. Because, if you do, there'll be…*consequences*."

The look in Trent's eyes changed.

James smiled.

The toilet flushed. "Ah." James pulled back the bedsheets, then slid a hand down into Trent's armpit and pulled out something red and swollen and throbbing. "If it helps to make you behave, Trent—" James held the Spider up for Trent to see, "—just think of me as your personal Dark Man."

He switched off the lights and closed the door as he left the bedroom, leaving Trent alone in the dark.

James managed to put a few steps between the bedroom and himself as Mum came out of the bathroom. She gave him a smile. "You look like a man on a mission. Looking forward to getting back to school tomorrow?"

James shrugged. "I just need to take something out for Tim."

"Haven't you already spoken to Tim?"

"It's that toy I borrowed from him." James held up the Spider, prodding it with his finger to make it look as though *he* was causing it to quiver. "Ten minutes? He's waiting outside."

"Five minutes." Mum hovered for a moment, then unexpectedly enveloped James in a bear hug. "You're a good kid, James," she said. "Things'll get better. You'll see."

"I know," James said, as he hugged Mum back.

Mister Black was already waiting in the street, tray clasped between gloved hands. He extended the tray, and James carefully deposited his Spider on top of the others. The rubbery mass briefly shuddered as one. Mister Black made a soft gurgling noise and twitched in ways that a human being couldn't possibly have managed. A stray ray of light from the setting sun momentarily lanced the darkness beneath Mister Black's hat, and James saw a flash of flesh-coloured latex with gaping black holes where eyes and a mouth should have been.

"The Spider…"

Mister Black slowly straightened up, face once again in darkness. "Yes?"

"It didn't just make Trent sick, did it? As he got sicker, the Spider got…healthier. It took something from him."

Mister Black nodded. "Well observed, Master James. Go on."

James considered. "Something it can only find in a certain sort of person. Something *you* need. The Spider collects it, and then you…" He gestured vaguely.

"Exactly so, Master James. And I thank you for assisting in the process." Mister Black hesitated. "I do hope these facts do not undermine the benefits of my service in your eyes?"

"Oh, no, not at all!"

There was a long pause.

"And…do you have a…*referral* for me?" Mister Black asked, at length.

James nodded again. "I was thinking about that." He turned and pointed further up the street. "Steven Moore, at number sixty-eight. He's not in my class, but we've talked. And sometimes I've been in the changing room getting into my PE kit at the same time he's getting out of his, and I've seen purple marks across his back that he tries to hide. The first time I thought they were birth marks, but they were in different places the next time." He paused. "Is that an okay *referral*?"

The brim of Mister Black's hat dipped again. "An *excellent* referral. Thank you, Master James."

"You're welcome."

"And with our contract completed, I must bid you farewell." Mister Black bowed slightly. then turned and began to glide smoothly away.

James stood for a moment, his mind swirling with questions, but the one that blurted from his lips was: "You're not really a monster, are you?"

Mister Black stopped abruptly, and James felt a sudden qualm, more afraid that he'd been rude than anything else.

After a moment, Mister Black turned back around to face James. "I suppose," he said, "that rather depends upon your *definition* of a monster. Don't you think?"

A beat. Then James nodded thoughtfully. "Yeah. I think you're right."

"Well then."

"Thank you!" James blurted.

"You are most welcome, Master James." Another small bow, and Mister Black turned and moved away. James watched him vanish into the lengthening shadows as the sun slipped below the horizon. Then he stood for a while longer, looking up at the stars, just enjoying the warm evening air and the sounds of other children playing in the street after dark.

The Mark of His Hands

Call it a confession, if you like…

We brought the capsule down among the hills three kilometres south-west of the Antonia Fortress, and immediately scanned the surrounding area for signs of incursion. For obvious reasons, Church had suspected this event would be an ideal target for extremists, but—much to our relief—we detected no anachronisms. Fulci and I donned our costumes, cloaked the capsule, and set out for the city.

Long before we reached the Jaffa Gate, we found ourselves caught up in an ever-increasing throng of locals heading in the same direction, and were virtually herded towards the marketplace as we entered the city. It was fortunate, then, that our secondary objective was to document that area; our primary objective being to observe the entombment itself, and whatever might occur afterwards.

You are surprised, of course, that Church would sanction such an operation. In the event we might disprove the story once and for all, what would happen to the faith upon which Church is founded? I myself had no such qualms; a Christian, yes, but a believer only in the historical facts of the event. My role on this expedition was as doctor and historian, Fulci's role being to verify the actuality—if any—of divine activity at this event, and good luck to him. We live in an age where most, like myself, take the stories not as truth but as parables, examples of the great things achievable through adherence to the moral codes He set down for us. To disprove the story would not be as devastating a revelation as one might expect, as Church well knew.

And besides, were the event shown to be *fact*… Ah! What *that* would mean!

The Sepulchre of Joseph lay half a kilometre back the way we had come, but He would not be taken there for many hours yet, giving us plenty of time to explore the marketplace, which had been hitherto undocumented. Our recordings would add valuable information to the existing files, giving Church a more complete picture of what had occurred in the city on this day.

And so we activated our nanocorders, and entered the market.

Those who have never jumped can scarce imagine the shock of immersing oneself in the culture of another era. For us, it was not merely the experience of unfamiliar surroundings; the immersions prepare you for that. What they don't prepare you for is the sensory overload that comes with the *reality* of being in another place and time. The very air smelt different—*tasted* different—as long-extinct species of plant and animal were boiled for broth. Peoples' skins had an odd texture. Clothes comprised strange fabrics, textures and colours. Strange languages, some of them perhaps never recorded for future study, assailed our ears. There was the sound of braying animals, sandals against stone, wind whistling through pre-Biblical architecture. The experience could not be any stranger had the capsule deposited us upon some alien world a billion light-years from Earth.

Less-experienced agents might have preferred to operate cloaked, but the best recordings come through interaction with the locals. And so Fulci and I strolled from stall to stall, chatting to vendors in the local dialect, never buying, politely rejecting the spruikers.

We had been there perhaps an hour when Fulci nudged me pointedly.

"Hey Savini, look—we've caught somebody's attention. Over there." He nodded surreptitiously.

Without turning my head, I glanced in the direction indicated. Piercing brown eyes glared back at me from an ebony countenance heavily lined by weather and age; teeth bared in a savage grin; torso thin, with painfully-hunched shoulders. "The negro in the tan tunic?"

"That's him. Giving us a good looking-over. Why so interested, I wonder?"

"A pickpocket, perhaps? Sizing us up?"

Fulci frowned. "Something almost...*malevolent* about the way he regards us."

I sighed inwardly. *Seeing demons in the shadows already.* "Unpleasant, I grant you, but—ah, he's realized we've seen him. Look, there he goes..."

Fulci nodded slowly. "Yes. Off to find an easier mark, no doubt." He did not sound convinced.

We wandered around for another hour or so, running a casual commentary between ourselves for the benefit of the 'corders. Occasionally, news runners would jostle their way through the crowds, shouting the progress of the event. Surprisingly few people took an interest—surprising only from our retrospective point-of-view, I suppose—but with each report a few ambled off in the direction of the city gates.

By noon, we felt that we had exhausted the possibilities of the market. The entombment was still several hours away, but there was no harm in getting there early.

We were making our way back to the gate, when Fulci grabbed my arm and hissed, "He's back!"

Startled, I looked around and caught sight of a familiar dark face flanking us from a few metres away, staring intently.

"There's something *wrong* about him." Fulci's face was troubled. "I can *feel* it. Can't you?"

I peered at the negro again. "Well, not *wrong*—but he's obviously no pickpocket. Look at the quality of his clothes. Besides, a good pickpocket wouldn't make his attention so obvious, and a bad pickpocket wouldn't live past the age of ten around here. A slave, perhaps. Or a freedman, more likely."

"Still doesn't explain his interest in us." Fulci shot me a look. "Perhaps he noticed something in our behaviour that marks us as…anachronistic?"

A chill ran down my back. "An enemy agent? You're getting paranoid."

Fulci didn't reply, but as we passed through the gate he drew me swiftly aside. We watched as the negro passed us by, vanishing amongst the stream of pedestrians heading towards Golgotha.

Relief flooded over me. "There you go—an agent wouldn't have allowed us to lose him so easily." I began feeling angry now, ashamed of how completely I'd allowed my imagination to run wild.

Fulci was still staring towards Golgotha. "We need to follow him."

"What?" I looked at him incredulously. "Fulci, we don't have time—"

"We have plenty of time. Anyway, what if you're wrong about the negro? You know the rules."

"This is pointless! The scan—" I stopped. Absence of anachronistic technology didn't guarantee an incursion-free zone. Enemy agents wouldn't need a staser to ensure the fall of Western civilisation—a locally made blade between the ribs before He had reached Golgotha would have been just as effective. But it was too late for that. To assassinate Him at this point would have virtually no impact upon futurity, given that He was already on the cross and only hours from death. Yet the rules were clear; any suspicion of incursion, no matter how slight, must be investigated.

And so we walked to Golgotha.

There was a fair crowd gathered when we reached the site, mostly camped out upon rugs, looking for all the world like picnickers on a Sunday outing. On the outskirts, people stood in huddled groups, socialising casually. A few solitary souls gazed at the spectacle below; faithful followers, no doubt, come to witness the death of their leader. Soldiers paced back and forth through the crowd, hands upon their hilts, alert for trouble. And in the centre of all this…

I had seen the excellent Romero-Coscarelli recordings, of course —indeed, like ourselves, those two would be mingling with the crowd at this very moment—but nothing could compare to seeing it with my own eyes.

He hung limply from the crucifix, His face blank and drooling. The agony must have shattered His mind long before we arrived. Massive wrought-iron pegs had been driven through His wrists, transfixing Him to the patibulum of the crucifix. The crown of thorns had lacerated His temples as effectively as the scourging had lacerated His back. Flies swarmed over Him, His body black with dried blood.

Below Him, on the edge of the crowd, a woman and a boy clung to one another, united in anguish. Mary and John. At His feet, soldiers played dice in the dust. Above their heads, the titulus—unreadable from where we stood, but I knew the words by heart.

Jesus of Nazareth, King of the Jews.

Tears stung my eyes. Can you imagine having to witness such an atrocity, knowing His suffering was *necessary* to forge the world we take for granted? With our technology we might have *prevented* this— and to even *think* such a thing, the insanity of it, brought me out in a cold sweat...

Fulci was weeping like a child, no doubt for different reasons than I. What was he thinking? That he gazed upon the personification of his God? That to witness this event somehow brought him closer to the Almighty? The thought irritated me immensely. Brushing my eyes dry with my sleeve, I glanced around the site until I found what I was searching for.

"There!" I pointed. "Do you see?"

Fulci blinked away his tears and looked. At the back of the crowd, off to the far left of the site, some enterprising food-vendors had pitched their tents, and in the shadow of one of the nearer stalls stood the negro, speaking animatedly with one of the soldiers. The soldier, armed with a long spear, was nodding slowly, which seemed to please the negro greatly. With one hand he rummaged under his tunic, producing a small bottle. With the other hand he held out a small cloth bag, hefting it invitingly. From the way its contents shifted, I guessed it to be full of coins. The soldier smiled, took the bag, then stepped back a few paces and lowered his spear, pointing it towards the negro's feet. The negro grinned, squatted down, and slowly drew the palm of his hand across the bladed edge of the spear, coating the metal in blood. Without bothering to bind the wound, he unstoppered the bottle and poured its liquid contents over the tip of the spear. The soldier watched the procedure with a blank look on his face; no doubt there were stranger sights to be seen elsewhere in the Empire. Apparently finished, the negro tucked the bottle back under his tunic, bowed to the soldier, and slipped away into the shadows.

Fulci stepped forward, obviously intending pursuit, but I stopped him. "Wait! Look!"

The soldier stood for a moment, gazing bemusedly at the tip of his spear. Then he raised the weapon and walked towards the crucifixes. Reaching the foot of His cross, the soldier exchanged a few words with the attendant guard, who stood back, nodding agreeably. The soldier carefully positioned himself beneath the cross, braced himself, then stabbed upwards with his spear.

There was a half-hearted cheer of approval from the section of the crowd nearest the action. Further back, somebody cried out as if in pain. Fulci shuddered.

There was no reaction from Him. Comatose, He had not even felt the wound that would hasten His death.

The pre-chrono historians had got it wrong, of course; they weren't supposed to have speared Him until *after* he died, as Romero and Coscarelli had gleefully pointed out. But now, a further development. "Interesting," I said. "Looks like the negro bribed the soldier to administer some sort of poison—though the whole thing had the look of a spell, didn't it? Blood and potions." I turned to regard Fulci. "Which, I submit, proves the negro *is* just some pagan local, not an enemy agent."

Fulci's expression was sullen. "Possibly. But we should still follow him. There's something *evil* going on here…"

And suddenly I understood.

I have never believed in Good and Evil, except as philosophical concepts, but Fulci certainly did. And far from believing the negro to be an enemy agent, he had obviously raised the idea purely to justify following an individual he believed to be supernaturally malign. And in doing *that*, he had landed a ringside view of the crucifixion—a diversion from our schedule that Church would never have condoned, had we not had the 'excuse' of surveilling a possible enemy agent.

My face burning with anger, I grasped Fulci's wrist as hard as I could, and was gratified to see his face blanch in pain. "When this operation is concluded," I hissed, "my official report will include a recommendation that you be submitted for disciplinary action!" Fulci opened his mouth to protest, but I cut him off. "Until then, we will adhere *exactly* to the mission schedule, and if you so much as *suggest* another deviation…" I left the threat hanging. In truth, I couldn't think of anything sufficiently terrible to threaten him with. "Is that understood?"

Fulci nodded tightly.

There was nothing more to say on the matter, so we turned and began walking north-west towards the Sepulchre of Joseph.

Soon after, darkness fell briefly in the middle of the afternoon. We stopped, bowing our heads, until the sun appeared again in the sky. Oddly, I felt nothing. Out of sight, out of mind. I did not look at Fulci to see his reaction.

By the time we arrived, a couple of guards—locals rather than soldiers, probably sent by the Pharisees—had already been posted, so we were obliged to cloak in order to enter the sepulchre. For some reason, one tends to think of His tomb as little more than a cave, but the interior was surprisingly spacious, perhaps ten by ten metres, with a beautifully carved sarcophagus resting upon a block of stone in the centre. We inspected the tomb for a while, for the benefit of the 'corders, then sat down on the clean-swept floor in the furthermost corner and waited.

After what seemed an eternity, we heard wailing and crying in the distance, growing slowly closer. Eventually, with the sounds of mourning right outside the tomb, two burly men entered carrying a body in a linen shroud. With obvious haste, they laid out the body inside the sarcophagus and left, pausing only to spit upon the floor. Moments later, with a great grinding sound, the light vanished.

We waited for a while, then stood up, de-cloaked and activated our night vision implants. Moving over to the body, I proceeded to tear the shroud open along the seam. The stench of preservative spices filled the tomb. Fulci gagged.

"Are you ready to do this?" I asked.

He nodded unenthusiastically.

"Okay, then." I cleared my throat. "Subject is male. Thirty-five years old. Medium build. Approximately one hundred and eighty centimetres tall." I pulled my medscan from the pouch at my belt, activated it, and held it over the body. He was definitely deceased, with no sign of pulse or respiration, and livor mortis had already begun to set in. Cause of death was orthostatic collapse, renal failure due to shock, and constriction of the heart by fluid in the pericardium. Blood loss due to multiple lacerations had also contributed. Not to mention… I moved the scan to cover the single, deep stab wound under the left-hand ribcage. "Hah."

"What?" I could hear the tremor in Fulci's voice. No doubt he objected to me treating His body so irreverently, and I derived a certain wicked pleasure from that.

"That stuff the negro put on the blade. Weird concoction. Puffer-fish venom, belladonna, a few herbal extracts. Highly narcotic, likely to induce psychotic delirium, slow respiration and heartbeat. Not very effective as a poison, but in His weakened state I suppose…" I glanced at the scan again. "Ah. Hemarthrosis. Ruptured blood vessels in his sweat glands." I gave Fulci a look. "Makes it look as though he was sweating blood prior to death."

Fulci nodded bleakly. Another mystery solved, for what it was worth.

"Nothing else unusual," I continued. "Healthy, for the age he lived in. And we already know what his last meal comprised—"

"Shh!" Fulci interrupted. "What was that?"

We stood motionless in the dark, listening.

"There!"

The sound of grinding stone, accompanied by the grunt of human exertion.

"Cloak!" whispered Fulci, and I followed his lead as the stone rolled aside. Of course, I had expected this intrusion—after all, if He had not risen from the dead then somebody must have taken the body —but I was surprised to find it occurring so soon. Another of my preconceptions, that the body had vanished *on* the third day. The report of the holy women three days hence would obviously result from sheer hysteria over the theft, rather than from anything they might actually see.

There was a pause. Then the jingle of coins, instantly explaining how the grave-robber had managed to get past the guards. And they, no doubt, would support the tale of resurrection as a means of hiding their involvement in the crime.

A figure appeared at the tomb entrance, face illuminated by the light of a flaming torch, and I felt Fulci stiffen beside me.

It was the negro.

He walked confidently into the tomb, torch raised high to illuminate the interior. Then he noticed the open shroud and stopped dead in his tracks, peering around suspiciously. He seemed to pause as his gaze swept over us—impossible, of course, as we were completely invisible—and I chided myself for an overactive imagination. And yet, for a moment, it truly seemed that his gaze met mine. I blinked, and this seemed to break the spell.

Muttering to himself, the negro moved over to the sarcophagus and examined the body intently, pulling the eyelids open to inspect the sightless orbs. Apparently satisfied by what he saw, he reached beneath his tunic and withdrew a small leather pouch, tied with a drawstring. Stepping back, he squatted down on his haunches, pulled the bag open, and tipped the contents out onto the floor: tiny bones—chicken bones, perhaps—which the negro began to arrange into a small circle. That done, he produced a piece of chalk, and began to draw something within the circle. It took me a moment to recognise the design.

A pentagram.

Immediately sensing what Fulci's reaction would be—to rush forward and destroy the offending scrawl with his sandal—I put out an arm to hold him back. The negro turned slightly, as though aware of movement behind him, grinned, and resumed his ceremony. We watched as he dug a palmful of yellow powder from a pouch at his waist, sprinkling it over the pentagram, then touched his torch to the circle. The powder began to smoke, a musty odour filling the room, and my head seemed to spin. Clearly the powder had narcotic properties.

The negro began to chant, a weird rhythmic babble that rose and fell in pitch and volume. And suddenly I felt a chill. Not a physical chill, but the feeling of something fundamentally *wrong*. Even as I berated myself for such foolishness, an unreasoning horror gripped me, and with it a sudden dread certainty that we had been *chosen* as players in this obscene ritual, lured in by our suspicion of the negro—for what dark purpose?

Numbed by fear, I was only vaguely aware of the chanting reaching a crescendo. The negro produced a handful of crimson powder from another pouch, and flung it into the smoking circle. There was a flash of violet flame, and the torch was suddenly extinguished.

At the same instant, my implant crashed. I spun around, groping blindly in the dark.

What occurred next—

Well, let me tell it as I remember.

As the powder ignited, the shadows in the tomb leapt and twisted, making the body in the sarcophagus appear to writhe with unholy life. Disoriented by the sudden darkness that followed I sought Fulci's arm, and heard a malicious cackling, followed by a scuttling sound. Somebody gasped loudly—Fulci, I assumed—although later I would think how it had sounded not so much like a gasp of shock, more a desperate sucking of breath into lungs bereft of oxygen. Then, the tearing of fabric, and the thud of unshod feet hitting the floor. The negro shouted something from the entrance.

I had a sudden sense of someone passing in front of me. And there was an odour; nothing I could identify exactly, although I was instantly reminded of the smell of old leaf-litter. Again, a chill. Physical, this time, as though a refrigerator door had opened before me. The hairs on the back of my neck prickled. *Something wrong.*

And then, something in the darkness beside me *hissed*.

At that, Fulci shrieked. Briefly. Choked into silence. Something heavy fell against me, knocking me to the floor. I lay there, hugging myself in terror. From outside the tomb came the sound of raised voices, frightened and querulous. Another shout from the negro.

Slow, listless footsteps shuffled past my head towards the entrance. The chill and the smell receded. Somebody outside screamed in fright, and I heard the sound of running feet vanishing into the distance.

A few seconds later my implant came back online…

And so, thirty years on—relatively speaking—here I am.

Comfortable, I grant you, my every desire attended to, bar one: freedom. But I understand. Church cannot take a chance upon my silence. If the full truth of this matter were ever revealed—

As I say, I am well looked-after, although I feel sure the subject matter of the reading material I request, which is always unquestioningly delivered, must raise eyebrows: Haitian history and culture, with particular focus upon the practice of so-called 'zombification'. I don't know quite what I am looking for, perhaps an indication that this practice can in some way be reconciled with God's great design. But the information in these documents is of little assistance, invariably describing a process by which the living attain the *appearance* of the dead, held in thrall to evil masters via administration of noxious compounds.

But He *was* dead.

And being dead…cannot die?

When I watch Omnet, images beamed in from across the globe, I find myself examining the faces. A cast of billions. And always I concentrate, searching desperately for a single visage that I hope, paradoxically, I shall never see…

I will die here, quite soon I think. And surely then I will find peace. If there is a God—and surely, if such supernatural evil can exist then so, I feel, must the Almighty—surely He, in his infinite mercy, will allow me to forget.

Forget the expression on Fulci's dead face, lying beside me as my implant came back online. The marks around his neck.

The mark of His hands.

Daddy's Always Right

Lucy presses her face up against the window, looking out at the planes as they trundle back and forth across the tarmac beyond. The plane Daddy says they'll be flying in sits still, just a few metres away.

"When can we get on, Daddy?" she asks impatiently.

Daddy, sitting in the row of seats just behind Lucy, says: "When they've finished cleaning up after the last lot of passengers, Sweetie. Won't be long now."

Lucy nods, satisfied. Daddy's always right.

Lucy turns and glances around the Departures Lounge. The old lady who smiled at her earlier is looking at her phone with a worried expression on her face. So are some of the other people, who Lucy thinks are probably going to be on the plane with them.

Lucy moves away from the window and sits next to Daddy. "Daddy?"

"Mm?" Daddy is reading his book, not really paying attention.

"Why is everyone looking scared?"

Daddy looks up from his book and glances around, then gives Lucy a smile. "There's some fighting going on in another country, and I think some people are just a little spooked. But it's nothing for you to worry about, okay Sweetie?"

Lucy smiles back. Daddy's always right.

Daddy goes back to his book.

A man sitting nearby jumps up, and walks quickly out of the lounge. Other people begin to do the same. The old lady starts to cry quietly. Lucy clutches Daddy's arm. The chairs vibrate suddenly, like when a truck goes past their home.

"What's that shaking, Daddy?"

Daddy doesn't even look up from his book this time. "Just planes landing, Sweetie."

Daddy's always right.

Lucy gets up and walks back to the window. People are beginning to run across the tarmac in all directions. A sudden blinding glare on the horizon makes her gasp and shield her eyes with both hands.

"Daddeee!" she says loudly, frightened now. "What's that light? What's that light, Daddy?"

Daddy sighs—Lucy can tell he still hasn't looked up from his book—and says in his familiar I'm-being-silly voice: "Well, I think it must be the end of the world, Sweetie."

Then everyone starts to scream. It's the last thing Lucy hears.

Daddy's always right.

Literality

They call me 'Bug-Eyed Monster' on account of my glasses. An expression of contempt and ridicule. But I'll show them what real BEMs can do: hunt, rend, feed...

"Transform me into a Bug-Eyed Monster!" Adrian commanded.

The demon smiled.

Adrian screamed as cockroaches churned from his bleeding sockets.

Like a Bug Underfoot

So when I finally get down to Centrelink, I find it's been trodden on the previous day. Piles of shattered masonry surround a giant paw-shaped depression where the building used to be. There's a security guy standing out front (guarding what?) so I ask him which Big Beastie did it. He says he doesn't know, and his expression says he doesn't care. I tell him I've come to fill out a dole form. He says I can't do it here. I say, well obviously, but can he tell me where I'm supposed to go now? He says he's fucked if he knows. I suggest he uses his walkie-talkie to ask someone who *does* know. He suggests I fuck off. Prick. At least he's being *paid* to do fuck-all. I'm taking out insurance on the next regular DJ gig I land, instead of assuming my employer's covered for damage by Giant Monsters. Act of God, my arse.

I walk all the way back to the flat. Shitbox car needs a new engine. Could've taken the bus, but that $4.50 might be buying me lunch next week. Should only be an hour-long walk, but when I get to Annandale I find it's in the process of getting stomped, with the Army blocking access and redirecting traffic all the way out to Balmain. Up ahead I can see the Beastie—something like a T-rex with tentacles—striding back and forth through the local shopping district. Back and forth, left to right, Beastie chased by helicopters, helicopters chased by Beastie. Don't recognise it. Might be a new one. I try chatting up the officer manning the roadblock: Any chance I could slip through? Beastie's not likely to notice a lone pedestrian. She says it's against orders. Translation: we don't want your next-of-kin to sue. So I take the two-hour detour, grinding my teeth as the noise of the Beastie's rampage slowly fades into the distance.

Can someone just tell me where the fuck they're coming from? Bastards appear out of nowhere, rampage through an improbably localised area, then vanish. Last month the scientists were talking about wormholes to alternate universes. Before that, it was genetic engineering. Wish they'd just admit they don't have a fucking clue, and concentrate on swatting the fuckers.

Dad blames the Japanese. For everything.

There's another bill shoved under the door when I get back (like they think I'll ignore it if they put it in the letterbox). Still can't bring myself to call the place 'home': a dark, mouldy, six-by-six metre hole with fleas in the carpet. And now I can't even afford the lousy $420 a week it costs to rent this shithole.

Just one thing makes it worth being here: Tina. Only been going out for three weeks—still at the never-stop-shagging stage—and she's already moved in. I could use some stress relief right now. Talk afterwards, get things off my chest. Great girl. But she's got a shift at the salon today, won't be back 'til after seven.

Still, gives me a chance to take stock of my finances, something I should've done as soon as I got retrenched. So: I know I've got about $200 left in my bank account. $5 in my wallet. Thought I had about $20 in change stashed in the kitchen drawer, but there's nothing there now. Must've frittered it away somehow. Practically broke. So—with no idea when I'm going to be able to put in a dole application—I figure it's time to hit the parents for a loan. Not before looking at every other possible option first, of course. I've already hocked most of my valuables. I'd consider working as an escort (I hear the money's good), but I know what Tina would say. Old-fashioned girl, and I love her for it.

Love?

Well, if it feels right…

So it's the parents. And honest-to-god, I would rather stick needles in my eyes than make this call, but I'm desperate.

I haven't used the phone in a week, and I'm surprised to find it still working. Then I remember it's the *power* that's on 'Final Demand'. The phone's on 'Reminder', and the gas isn't due for two weeks. Haven't lived in a place fitted with gas before, and I don't like it. It's bad enough the service gets shut down every time the pipeline gets stomped, but the next time some fire-breathing Beastie strolls past, the whole place could go up. The building superintendent—old guy living downstairs—reckons the agent's been promising to switch to electric any day now. Sure. And then the rent'll skyrocket to cover the cost.

The call to Melbourne takes bloody ages to get through. A recorded voice waffles on about how they're experiencing delays due to circumstances beyond their control; code-speak for 'some fucking huge mutant reptile just burned our exchange to the ground'. But eventually the phone rings.

Dad answers. Mum I can get around without too much of a lecture, but Dad's a tough nut. Lately he seems to *expect* me to fuck up, as if I ceased to be an adult the moment I left his field of supervision. So I just get straight to the point and ask for a loan, promising to pay him back ASAP.

"Well," he says, "it's not as if we have that sort of money just lying around. And you never paid back the removalist's fee to Sydney." Ouch. We both know he's never getting *that* money back.

"Listen," I say, "I *am* looking for work. There's just nothing available at the moment." All the local clubs have resident DJs booked already. But Sydney's a party town. Something'll come up.

"Local papers are full of ads for waitstaff. I imagine it's the same in Sydney."

Boom.

The room shakes slightly. Sirens begin to wail in the distance.

"Look, if I've gotta wait tables to pay the rent, that's fine," I lie. "But until I *find* a waiting job, I still need a loan."

Boom.

A sigh. "How much did you say you needed?" I tell him again. "Just about enough to pay off your debts and get back home." *Where we can keep an eye on you.*

BOOM.

Car alarms go off nearby.

It's like talking to a brick wall. He's always been like this; it doesn't matter what I say, nothing's going to change his view. So we argue round in circles, going over the same ground again and again, until I blow my top. But I *need* that loan, so I try to keep my cool. "Dad, I can't just move back to Melbourne. I live in Sydney now." Lame. "Something's bound to come along soon."

BOOM.

Plaster dust trickles from the ceiling.

So what now? Maybe the famous 'if only you'd worked harder at school' speech? Or 'if only you'd put away some savings before moving out'? But instead, Dad asks what all the noise is at my end. I tell him. He goes quiet for a moment, then tells me I'm always welcome back home, and he'll transfer the funds right away. Thanks Dad, gotta go, can't afford to use the phone right now. I hang up, angry and ashamed.

BOOM!

The floor rolls under my feet. An ear-splitting screech rattles cracked panes. Against my better judgement I step to the window, and catch a glimpse of the Beastie as it strides past the flat. Not the Annandale-smasher, but about the same size, big as an office block. Massive legs pound holes in the road. Upper limbs flail like those of some nightmare *Thunderbirds* puppet. Rage-reddened eyeballs roll above a slavering, snaggle-toothed maw. Noxious secretions bubble between immense scales. Dog-sized parasitic insects skitter across heaving flanks. The smell is overpowering; sickly-sweet and cloying, like the reptile house at the zoo.

Fighter jets roar overhead. The Beastie screams again. A long, spiked tail lashes out, and I jump back. *Crunch.* The building shakes, powdered masonry fogging the air.

And then it's gone.

Boom. Quieter now. The stench fades, but now there's another smell, heady and choking, like methylated spirits. *Shit!* I throw open the window, then check the stove, but I can't tell whether it's leaking or not. The smell slowly dissipates, but I'm still rattled. Do I need to call someone? Tina would know what to do. Maybe one of the neighbours?

I open the front door. Most of the other tenants are out on the stairwell already. The super's just coming back inside to tell everyone the Beastie's moving away towards Liverpool Road. Everybody nods, retreating back into their hovels without comment.

The old guy catches my eye. "Close one, eh? *Arrakis*, he's a nasty one." He smiles self-consciously. "Grandkids collect the trading cards."

"I think I've got a gas leak."

"Want me to give the gas company a call?"

"Cheers." I nod and start to close the door.

"Shame about the building, isn't it?"

"Yeah. Still, could've brought the whole place down, eh?"

"No, I mean… Oh." He squirms. "Didn't you get the letter from council?"

I shake my head. I probably did, but I always bin council correspondence. It's usually campaign crap. "Why, what's up?"

"They're going to knock the building down. Cracks in the foundations, from all the monsters stomping around. Not safe anymore."

The situation suddenly feels unreal, like I'm having a bad dream. "But—what happens to *us?*"

He shrugs. "I've lived here twenty-five years, you know…"

"Yeah, well," I say, and begin to shut the door again.

"Oh, by the way," he says quickly, "there were some gentlemen here earlier, asked me to tell you—"

Debt-collectors. Great. I shut the door.

Fuck. *Fuck.*

The phone rings. Christ! Now what?

It's the cops.

"Do you know a girl named Tina Ashton?"

The back of my neck begins to prickle. "She's my girlfriend—is she okay?"

"Ah, listen mate, we've arrested her in connection with a series of thefts and frauds."

Boom.

My lip curls involuntarily. "Nah, listen, there must be some kind of mistake—"

"Yeah, you're about the fifth bloke I've heard that from. We've been after her for ages. Moves in with a bloke, gives him some tall story about her circumstances, then pisses off with his cash."

Boom.

"Had any money go missing? Cheques?"

"I…don't know."

"Could you take a look for me?"

I put the phone down and pull my chequebook out of the (suspiciously) change-free kitchen drawer. The book looks intact. I smirk with relief. Then I notice a sliver-thin gap at the back of the tightly-bound stack of cheques. My throat constricts. I flick to the back of the book. A single tell-tale fleck of paper peeks out from the spine, where several cheques have been torn out, stub and all.

Boom.

I pause, feeling nauseated. My head seems to spin. Then I pick up the phone again. "Ah…"

"Thought so," says the cop. "Probably drawn against your account with a forged signature. Better check with your bank. I bet she's cleared you out…"

His voice drones on, but my ears are full of white noise.

Boom.

"…need you to come in and make a statement."

Tears are streaming down my cheeks.

"You there, mate?"

I draw a shuddering breath. "I…I mean, are you *sure?* I was going to meet her folks next week—"

The cop laughs explosively.

"Aw, sorry mate, I'm not laughing at *you*. It's just that we've been after this girl for that long, and some of the bullshit stories she's been telling… Her folks are *dead*, mate. Died when Wollongong got stomped."

BOOM.

"So when you reckon you could come in and make a statement?"

With the car out of commission, I beg a lift.

"Sure, mate. We'll get someone over tomorrow." A pause. "By the way—I know this is a personal question, but…you *have* been sleeping with her, I s'pose?"

"Yes..?"

"Okay. Look, ah, you should get an AIDS test."

I can't think of anything to say.

BOOM.

The room trembles as I hang up the phone. My heart pounds, breath coming in short, sharp gasps. Numbness grips me, adrenalin icing my veins. I feel light-headed and weak. The room seems to fade, patchy contrasts of light and shade pressing in, muffling the outside world.

BOOM!

A dull shriek pierces the fog. The window darkens. Helicopters buzz angrily overhead. The smell of alien flesh and petroleum combines to nauseating effect.

I *loved* her. Only three weeks, but—

And now—

It hits without warning, like a tsunami. Rage. White heat burns my face. I stagger, trying to scream, choking as my mouth fills with spittle. I want to tear the room apart. I want to crush, destroy, kill. Until everything lies in ruin.

Until the pain goes away.

But the rage is too great; I writhe impotently under its weight, unable to move, unable to breathe—

BOOM!

The impact releases me. Shrieking my hatred, I run to the door, slam it open, pound down the stairs to the street and out into the middle of the road. I stand there, shaking uncontrollably, mucus bubbling from my eyes, nose and mouth; the Hulk in trendy clubwear, roaring defiance at this shitpile of a world, fists clenched, ready to lay waste to all before me.

"Come on, you fuckers! You fucking bastards! Come on! Come on, I'll fucking kill *you, you fucking bastards! Argh!"*

The Beastie looms over me, unconcerned, perhaps not even aware, as if I were a bug underfoot.

The thought enrages me beyond all reason. I scream again, ready to sink my nails into reptilian flesh—

This, I suddenly realise, is the Beasties' secret. Rage. Raw emotion, providing power enough to move monsters through time and space, to fuel rampages through brick and mortar and steel, to shield against the arsenals of humankind, the agonies of everyday life—

I grin savagely, glaring upwards, arms thrown wide in open challenge.

"Have a go, you fucker! Come on, have a fucking go! I'll rip your fucking head off! Come on—do your fucking worst!"

A mighty foot descends, blotting out the world.

Moth

The car behind is flashing its headlights, so Henry obligingly pulls over. The two creatures that leap from the other car are not human. They are, however, very fast. As slavering jaws close in, Henry hears one remark to the other, "See? They can't resist the lights."

Bad Meat

"Bad meat!"

Ruby just won't stop saying it, slurring her words like some kind of retard, and at this precise moment *that's* what's really freaking Ted out, despite everything else that's just happened. It's only when he hears her shamble down the stairs after him that he thinks this maybe has something to do with all that bullshit on TV about dead folk turning into mindless, walking cannibals. Maybe if he'd made the connection earlier he would have run out the front door and down to Mike's, or something, instead of down to the basement to hide in the disused freezer in the corner. Not his smartest move ever, he's forced to admit, but he is pretty drunk and freaked out. He's got a finger pushed out under the padded seal running around the inside of the lid so it can't close and smother him, so he should be okay, as long as she doesn't look in the freezer.

"Bad meat!"

So maybe he'll be okay if he keeps real quiet, assuming that dead people can even hear, of course.

He'd had to show her Consequences before, of course. But this time he'd barely tapped her when she insisted the steak couldn't have been off *("Don't tell me it's not bad meat, you stupid cow!")*. She'd spun away, down onto the glass-topped coffee-table, and instantly bled out around the massive shard through her neck. He guessed it was a combination of shock and booze that made him just sit right down again and watch TV, despite all the blood everywhere. Waiting for her to move, like she always did after a while.

"Bad meat!"

When she still hadn't moved ten minutes later he began to worry that maybe he was going to get in some trouble over this. But then she began to stir, so he relaxed, and the next thing he knew she was all over him, trying to sink her teeth into his face. So he popped her one, but good, and she kept coming at him, so he landed a real haymaker. She staggered a bit, then came at him again. And that's when Ted's nerve went, because Ruby could never brush off a blow like that, so he'd run down to the basement and jumped straight into the freezer without even thinking about it, and maybe that's because Ted's stepdad had kept a disused, refrigerator in the shed when Ted was young, where the Old Man never thought to look when he was in one of his moods.

"Bad meat!"

She's in the basement now, and how the fuck is he going to get out of this one? Ted recalls the TV saying something about smashing the brain to put them down, and immediately wishes he'd kept a few more blunt instruments around the house, but of course he'd never before needed any weapon other than his fists. There may be a baseball bat somewhere in the basement, if he can get to it before she gets to him, because that's the other thing he's just remembered from the TV: don't let them bite you, or scratch you, or even spit in your eye, because that's how it spreads to living folk.

"Bad meat!"

She won't shut up, going on about bad meat like she can only remember the last thing he said to her, or (the thought occurs) maybe she's finally admitting that the meat was bad, or—*hey!*—maybe it's the meat that's carrying the virus, and suddenly Ted thinks that, far from getting into trouble (and he can always say she was already dead when he hit her, can't he?), he could come out of this a hero if he tells the authorities it's in the meat—

—and then the lid of the freezer flies up, and Ruby looks down at Ted, jammed into the corner of the freezer, and grins in a way that makes him think, briefly, that maybe these things aren't as mindless as the TV says.

"*Bad* meat!" she slurs, and the emphasis is unmistakable.

Confessions of a Pod Person

I am out in the front garden, watering the hedge, when Jim Taylor comes walking by, and the part of me that is still Chuck McKenzie remembers to wave and say hi.

Jim stops and leans on the front gate—just like the real Jim Taylor would have done—and comments on how the hedge is coming along nicely. I nod and say yes, it certainly is. Jim says, it must be all the good weather we've been having. I agree, but note that the forecast is predicting rain. Ah well, says Jim, rain's as good for the garden as sun. So why does it rain on the footpath? I ask, and we both laugh. As always.

We have had this conversation many times before. It is important that we have done so and continue to do so, because the real Jim Taylor and Chuck McKenzie had these sort of conversations on a regular basis, and with the invasion over it is more important now than ever before that the few of Us remaining continue to blend in.

"Chuck?"

Jim and I turn towards the house. Megan is standing on the porch, smiling, her hand placed carefully against the doorframe. She is wearing a light cotton dress that moves slightly with the breeze, and I think to myself that she looks very beautiful…

I frown. The fact that she is beautiful should not have occurred to me, since it is irrelevant to our survival. I am a little concerned about this—at least, I remember how concern would have felt to Chuck. This sort of thing has occurred more and more frequently over the past few months. Emotive responses. And this, of course, is impossible.

"Chuck?"

I call back: yes, I'm here.

"Is that Jim with you? Hi Jim!"

Jim smiles, and remarks that there is no fooling her, and asks how she is doing.

She shrugs. "Yeah, not bad. Listen, I'm sorry to break up the party, Jim, but I need Chuck to come and help me get dinner ready."

Be right there, I say. Megan nods, and carefully makes her way back inside. I turn to Jim. Duty calls, I say. Is that what you call her? he says. And we laugh. I turn off the tap, then move towards the house, half-turning to wave goodbye to Jim. Jim waves back. Okay Chuck, he says, I'll see you later. Only if I don't see you first, I say. And laugh.

Jim fixes me with a blank stare. I can read that look clearly. It says: *What the hell was that?*

I cannot answer. Chuck McKenzie never made that joke. It is something new. Where did it come from?

Jim is still looking at me, so I quickly mention—as Chuck would have done—that I might go down to the local bar a little later on. Will he be there? Jim's smile returns, though his eyes remain blank. True emotion never touches our eyes. Family members tend to notice this. They begin to suspect. Which would not normally have been a long-term problem, except that the pods left before some of Us could replace our families. Most of Us in this situation are now living alone— separated, divorced, or with spouses institutionalised. A couple of Us still live with our unreplaced families, but relations are tense.

I am very lucky to have someone like Megan.

Jim smiles warmly, his eyes still blank. I'll see you at the bar then, he says, and walks off.

I watch him go, feeling unaccountably disturbed, then go into the house to help prepare dinner.

When dinner is over, and I have done the washing up and switched on the radio for Megan, I retreat to my study to do some writing. I sit before my laptop, fingers tapping lightly over the keyboard, pouring out a dry catalogue of the events of the day. Chuck used to do this during bouts of writer's block; to keep his fingers agile, he would say. But now it is the only sort of writing I am capable of. Like actors, we take on the appearance, mannerisms and memories of those we replace. Unlike actors, we can work *only* with the material provided. There is no improvising. It is a survival strategy which has served Us well for countless millennia. To go beyond the bounds of what is *known* to be the accepted behaviour of those we replace would be to draw attention, to invite discovery. Everything we do is a routine composed entirely of snippets of someone else's life, re-enacted in random order as required.

There is a tentative knock, and Megan appears in the doorway. "How's it coming along?"

Not so great, I say. Writer's block. Just knocking out gibberish.

This was Chuck's standard reply during periods of creative frustration, but I know the response is beginning to wear thin. Chuck McKenzie has not done any real writing for the last three years: not since that night when Megan went to stay with her mother, and Chuck fell asleep on the couch downstairs, next to the open window.

Megan nods understandingly, but I sense her worry. Money has not been an issue before. Three bestsellers prior to replacement have provided well. But the royalties will not keep coming in forever. Chuck needs to produce some new work soon, or find an alternate line of work, and the latter is not an option—writing is all Chuck knew, is all *I* know. And my inability to write anything original puts me in the most awkward position of any of Us. As a baker, or an accountant, or a mechanic, I could have effortlessly maintained the pretence, not needing to know or do anything new. A writer, however, must produce new, fresh, original work to survive. Creativity. Imagination. Initiative. And we have none of these.

I sigh, and ask Megan if she would mind me ducking out to the bar for an hour or so to have a few drinks with the boys.

She dazzles me with a smile. "Sure, hon. I'll be fine."

Are you sure? I ask. Can I get you anything before I go?

She waves me away. "I'm not an invalid. I'll be fine. Say hi to the guys for me."

I assure her I'll do just that, then grab my coat and wander down the road.

The sky is very clear tonight, and the stars are just beginning to appear. Chuck would have stopped to appreciate them, so I do, and wonder where the pods are now.

I remember the night we stood in the field at the outskirts of town, united in our pursuit of the town doctor who had resisted our efforts to replace him. He had flooded the field with petrol, igniting the liquid as we closed in. The pods responded instinctively, twisting free of the soil and floating up into the sky. Earth had proven itself too hostile. Maybe the next thousand worlds will also be too hostile. Just one suitable world will do, where conditions allow the pods to settle and grow. I remember standing with the others, looking up at the sky. Then we all turned and went back to our homes. There was nothing else to do. The doctor was not harmed. There was no point in retribution. The invasion had failed, and we who were left had no choice but to go back to our routines. The whole point of our mode of existence is to survive wherever we are able. The doctor still has a practice in town. Like Us, he maintains the pretence that all is normal. How could he do otherwise? Who would believe his story?

And besides, he knows that all he has to do is wait.

We are not perfect replicas. We will produce no children, and all of Us will be dead within the next two years. Again, this is our accepted mode of existence. It has always been this way. We live, we die, we cultivate the pods, which carry Us on to other worlds. Our race goes on.

And yet, recently I have been having…concerns. Chuck McKenzie was only thirty when I replaced him. He might have lived to the age of seventy, or longer. And I have begun to think—to *feel*—that a five-year lifespan is…not enough.

It is impossible, of course, for me to think such things. Such thoughts could only have come from Chuck's own memory.

But I have no recollection of Chuck ever considering the issue of his own mortality…

I enter the bar and pause, pretending to look around for the others. Of course, I know exactly where they will be—over in the corner booth by the potted palm. Jim Taylor, Steve Brown, Rick Collins and Alan Hargreaves. I peer into the gloom, as if trying to make sure it is really them, and Jim waves cheerily at me. I walk over, sit down next to Alan, and we all exchange pleasantries.

We took the liberty of ordering you a beer, says Steve.

Cheers, I say, the next round's mine.

Rick was just about to tell us a joke, says Alan. Go on, Rick.

So Rick tells the joke about the nun and the banana, while we all pretend to hear it for the first time—except for Alan, who nods and says he has heard this one, but lets Rick finish anyway. We all laugh dutifully as Rick gives us the punch line.

A few unreplaced locals sitting at nearby tables give Us wary looks. Many of the townsfolk know that something is not right about Us. Most of them do not truly suspect what we are, but they know we are not who we pretend to be. Recently, I have been wondering if there is any point in continuing the pretence. But I can also see how the truth might push some of these people over the edge.

Tim Stratton, one of the bar attendants, comes to the table bearing five schooners of beer on a tray. He carefully puts the tray down and lets Us take our drinks. "Twenty bucks," he says. Jim pays. Tim does not make eye contact. He is obviously nervous, but conducts himself as normally as possible. It occurs to me that human beings often seem to cope with extreme situations simply by sticking to their regular routines, drawing comfort from that sense of normality.

Maybe we are not so different, Us and them.

I ask Tim how he is doing. He looks up, startled.

"Okay, I guess," he mutters.

The Others give me a look. I ignore them, and—insanely—place my hand on Tim's forearm. Tim, I say, everything's okay. I mean that. There's no need to be afraid—

The others stare, their eyes black as tar.

Tim shakes his arm free and staggers back a few paces. He takes a deep breath, then hisses: *"I know what you are!"*

Jim leans forward. Do you? he asks, coldly.

Tim stumbles away, his face grey.

I glare at the others. What did you do that for? I ask furiously. They stop laughing, faces blank. None of Us get mad anymore, not even in pretence, so my outburst takes them by surprise.

After a moment Jim asks what is wrong with me.

What is wrong with *me?* I ask. What the hell is wrong with *you?* It might help if people were not scared of Us!

The others stare at me. I fume silently, taking a big swig of beer. The others exchange looks.

You know, says Jim eventually, Chuck was telling me a new joke today. *A new joke.*

Alan looks around to ensure that nobody is listening in, then pushes his face towards mine. What is going on? he asks.

I do not know, I say. I just feel—

Feel? asks Jim.

There is a long silence.

Something odd, I say, gazing into my beer. I am having…episodes. As though I can actually *feel* the emotion. Have any of you—?

I look up, and can see from their expressions that they have not.

The thing is, I say, these are not Chuck's memories. These emotive responses are not his.

The others say nothing.

I am…*changing*, I say.

The others exchange another look. Jim leans forward. The expression on his face is pained, as though the act of questioning my statement causes him physical discomfort. How? he asks.

The answer has been brewing at the back of my mind for some time now, and I have been doing my best to ignore it. But it is as if Jim's question has thrown a switch, and the words are out of my mouth before I can stop them.

I think I am evolving, I say.

Steve switches back into Steve mode, smirks and stands. I'm outta here, he says, and gives me a contemptuous look. You're *nuts*, buddy! He stalks out of the pub. This, at least, is part of the regular routine. Steve always was an aggressive drunk. Rick goes with him, casting a stony look back as he leaves.

Alan and Jim remain, staring at me. I stare back.

If the invasion had not failed, if the entire town had been replaced, these guys would be content to dispense with the act altogether. With no one left to threaten our survival, the routines would cease to be useful. No work would be done, nothing would be cleaned, or maintained, or rebuilt. The roads would fall into disrepair, isolating the town from the outside world. We would simply *exist*—eating, sleeping, excreting—until we died, leaving behind a ghost town. The thought makes me…*angry*.

Evolving, says Alan, flatly.

Well? I say, defensively. We are at the pinnacle of evolution, universally. We evolved to that level in order to survive. So if an invasion fails—if the option to leave does not exist for we who are replacements—well, who is to say we could not *individually* evolve further in order to survive?

Jim leans forward again. *I* say, he says, because it has never happened before. Ever.

I say, well, absence of proof is not proof of absence, and Jim gives me another blank look because that is not something that Chuck would ever have said. Shaking my head in frustration, I drain my glass and stand. I dig a few crumpled notes from my pocket and toss them on the table. That should cover the next round, I say. Jim starts to speak, but I cut him off, saying that I want to get back home to my wife. And I actually mean it.

Jim must see something in my face that conveys this, because he sits back, looking almost frightened. Something passes between Us. Somehow, we know that this routine is over. We will not be drinking together again. Not like this, anyway—the whole gang together. That was Chuck's thing. But somehow, impossibly, I am no longer the person I replaced.

I am…*me.*

Of course, something of the original Chuck McKenzie remains; thirty years of memory providing a foundation to fall back upon when necessary. I do that now, nodding amiably to Jim and Alan as I head towards the door. Cheers guys, I say, loud enough for those sitting nearby to hear. I'll catch you later.

It is a comparatively small lie, all things considered.

Just me, I call out as I arrive home. Getting no response, I stick my head around the living room doorway and see Megan curled up on the couch, asleep. I tiptoe across the room and turn off the radio, careful not to disturb her, then go to my study. I open the laptop, sit back in my chair and stare at the screen, at the diary I was working on earlier. I stare at it for a very long time, thinking about what has occurred tonight.

Part of me is…relieved, I suppose. At least, I remember relief feeling like this. Everything is out in the open—amongst Us, at least—

and I have finally been able to rationalise what is happening to me. But a knot of tension remains in my stomach. I have a major decision to make. A choice. To go on as before, operating safely as an automaton, which offers no hope for what little future I have. Or, to put my future in my own hands. To show *initiative*.

Either is a frightening prospect.

I continue to stare at the screen, gripped by a growing sense of frustration. One idea. Just one new idea. That is all I need. One lousy idea for a book…

Nothing.

For the first time in my short life I *feel* like crying. I look at the diary—dry, pointless words on the screen. I bury my face in my hands. I cannot do it. No creativity. And yet, that joke I told Jim earlier—that had to come from *somewhere*. I stare at the screen again, trying to find a story amongst the lines of meaningless drivel.

Still nothing.

I look at the bookshelf against the far wall. A jumble of hardbacks and paperbacks, science-fiction and action bestsellers, scientific references, writing textbooks, and biographies. Chuck had a fondness for biographies, and there is an eclectic mix of them on the shelf. Pop stars, politicians, sporting celebrities and business figures: their lives laid out in prose, dry facts presented in a style approximating fiction...

I look back at the screen, thinking. After a moment, I move the cursor and double-click the very first file comprising my diary of the last three years. I lean forward, examining the old words intently. The naked truth, completely ungarnished. And dangerous. If anyone from outside town were to recognize the names of people and places mentioned here…

I sigh. Too dangerous.

Unless…

If I were to alter *this* sequence of events, change *these* names... Not a fabrication, exactly. More…restructuring the truth.

Almost automatically, my fingers begin flickering across the keyboard.

"Chuck?"

I turn. Megan stands in the doorway, her eyes heavy with sleep. Right here, I say.

"I didn't hear you come in," she says. "You coming to bed?"

Soon, I say.

"Finishing up that gibberish you were working on?"

No, I say, I'm…working on a new book.

"Really?"

Yes, I say. Just came to me today. It's—I hesitate, then go on—it's about aliens who invade a small town. The first ones to arrive take over the bodies of the townsfolk, then the invasion fails, and the rest of the story is about what happens to the aliens who are left behind.

She makes a face. "Sounds creepy. Horror story? Or science fiction?"

I pause, considering carefully. No, I say. I actually thought of it as a romance novel. Sort of.

She nods, but looks a little confused.

I think I'll give Sarah Kernot a call tomorrow, I say. See if I can sell this.

Megan looks surprised, but pleased. Sarah is Chuck's agent, to whom he hasn't spoken in three years. "Really? That's excellent!"

Just give me fifteen minutes more on this, and I'll come to bed, I say.

She smiles. "Okay. Fifteen minutes."

Do you need a hand getting upstairs? I ask.

"No," she says. "I'll be fine." She turns away, feeling for the handrail that runs along the hallway and up the stairwell.

"I love you," I say. And mean it.

She pauses, then turns back to face me. Her sightless eyes fix upon a spot on the wall just above my head. "I love you too," she says softly, then adds: "Come to bed soon, and I'll show you how much."

I watch her go, then turn back to the laptop. I look at the words on the screen. There is some good stuff here—stuff I can work with.

Tomorrow.

I reach out and close the laptop. Chuck McKenzie, in the grip of inspiration, would have carried on working into the small hours of the morning. But I am not Chuck McKenzie. Nor am I any longer a mere facsimile. I am something different. Something new. What happens to me now is largely up to me. My life, my decisions.

Yes, I think. The story can definitely wait until tomorrow. Right now, I want to be with my wife.

Of course, there will be no children. And one day soon my wife will wake to find my lifeless body lying beside her in bed.

I think about that for a moment.

Of course…there *is* the possibility of adoption, I suppose. Or IVF. Using donor sperm. And if, as I suspect, that five-year lifespan is due as much to our dogged adherence to survival protocol as to anything biological…

Well, then maybe—*maybe*—I can beat this thing simply by *wanting* to go on.

It is worth a try. What do I have to lose? What might I have to gain? Thirty years more? Ten? Five? It doesn't matter. *More time* is all that is important. More time to write. To live. To be with my wife.

Moving to the study door, I switch off the light and make my way upstairs.

I can do this. I *know* I can do this.

No, I think.

We can do this. Megan and I. Together.

Retail Therapy

Quentin started, mortified by the immediate realisation that he'd actually nodded off on the job. Panicked and disoriented, he stared wildly around the shop.

Alone.

Perspiration trickled into his eyes, and he mopped it away with an already sweat-stained shirt cuff. *Bloody heat!* Hottest summer on record, and here he was stuck in a *lighting shop*, for Chrissake, dressed in constrictive business attire, surrounded by hundreds of oyster fittings, desk lights, standard lamps, halogens, bloody bathroom *heat-lamps* for Chrissake, all blazing away, sapping his will to stay awake. Days like this, Quentin regretted ever buying the bloody business. Would have been okay if the place did well enough for him to hire some staff, give him a chance to get out on the road and maybe visit a few building sites, drum up some corporate customers. The shop was supposed to be an investment. Instead, he'd just wound up buying himself a bloody job.

Deep in his stomach, his ulcer began to throb painfully. He knew it was an ulcer, no matter what his doctor said. "Heartburn," the quack had opined. "Brought on by stress, which is also obviously making you very angry. And you're repressing that anger. If you keep bottling it up like this, you're liable to burst a blood vessel. Here's a referral for a very good therapist, who'll tell you the same thing."

Quentin took a deep breath. *Relax. Just stick to the plan; good prices, great customer service. Things'll turn around—*

Something moved at the back of the shop.

Quentin started again, then leaned forward across the counter, squinting through sweat-stung eyes. There, by the tiffany lamp display…

Quentin glanced at the clock hanging on the wall opposite. 4.55 pm. He frowned irritably. *Always the bloody way! Not a single sale all day, then somebody walks in five minutes before closing time and wants to browse!* Immediately, he felt a pang of guilt. *That's a terrible attitude!* Quentin sighed, wiped the sweat from his brow, straightened his tie, and began to step out from behind the counter. Then he paused.

How the hell had a customer managed to walk past the counter to the back of the shop without him noticing?

You were asleep!

The burning sensation in Quentin's stomach intensified. He must have been slumped over the counter, dead to the world, when the customer walked in. *So much for customer service.* He looked down at himself; a sweaty, rumpled little man. *Dammit!* He tried to smooth down the front of his shirt with his hand, and the cotton stuck in great ugly patches to his sweat-slicked abdomen. *Bugger!* Well, he'd simply have to dazzle with service. Quentin took a deep breath, forced a pleasant smile, and moved towards the customer.

The customer didn't register Quentin's approach, his attention focussed instead upon the small leadlight table lamp he was holding. Grey-blue eyes peered from a round, pale face, which seemed to float balloon-like above the collar of the customer's dun-coloured overcoat. Grubby, pallid hands flipped the lamp carelessly back and forth with no apparent regard for its fragility as the customer examined the item from every possible angle. His expression was one of dismissive contempt.

"Hello there. May I help you?" asked Quentin, politely.

The customer gave no indication he had heard the query.

Quentin edged further into the customer's line-of-sight. "Can I help you there?"

The customer raised his head, met Quentin's gaze momentarily, then returned to his examination of the lamp.

Dismissed. Quentin felt the muscles in his neck tighten. "Looking for anything in particular?"

Nothing. Not even a flicker of acknowledgement.

Rude. Problem customer. As if on cue, the pain in Quentin's stomach became more acute. Quentin winced, narrowing his eyes. Sweat blurred his vision. *Bloody heat!*

"No," the customer muttered, apparently to himself. "No—that won't do at all." His voice was high and nasal, instantly annoying. Bending, he thrust the lamp roughly back down onto the mirrored display table. There was a distinct *ting!* as the shade impacted against a neighbouring lamp.

Quentin twitched. *Clumsy idiot!* He resisted the urge to grab the lamp and inspect it. Insurance would cover any breakages, but charging the customer for damages would be far more satisfying. *Calm down! The heat's making you crazy! Don't alienate yourself from the customer before you've even got a dialogue going! Fastest way to lose a sale...*

The customer straightened up and turned towards Quentin, revealing a formal dinner suit beneath the overcoat. The sort of ensemble favoured by opera-goers on chilly nights. Ridiculous, given the heat. Not to mention pretentious. Quentin glanced at the clock. 5.05 pm. Conscious of the perspiration gathering once again on his brow, he stuck out his bottom lip and directed a cooling breath upwards, wishing—not for the first time—that he sold fans instead of lights.

The customer didn't seem bothered by the heat, however. Having glanced dismissively around the interior of the shop, his gaze finally fixed upon a point exactly two centimetres below Quentin's face.

Is he looking at my collar? Is my tie straight? Quentin smiled nervously.

"Got any hanging lights?" The customer's tone suggested complete disinterest in however Quentin might respond.

Quentin blinked, then made a show of looking around at the dozens of lights hanging from the ceiling. "Pendant lights? Yes, we certainly do."

The customer glanced upwards. "Hmm." He reached up and touched the white frosted shade of the nearest pendant, leaving a greasy thumb-print on the glass.

Quentin stifled a burp as bile rose painfully in his gullet. *Maybe the quack's right—heartburn, brought on by stress.* He swallowed hard, and the discomfort subsided.

The customer continued to paw the fixture for a moment, then grabbed at the price tag hanging from the light. "How much is this?"

Quentin sighed inwardly. "Let's see…" He reached out and placed his finger against the ticket, indicating the price boldly printed in thick, red numerals. "There we go…" He glanced at the customer, who continued to stare blankly at the ticket. "One-hundred and ninety-nine dollars."

The customer hurriedly released the ticket as if it were diseased. "I'm sure you can do better on the price." It was not a question.

Quentin's nostrils flared. Plenty of people asked for discounts; for cash, for bulk purchases, for tradesmen. Haggling was no longer a practice restricted to the markets of Chinatown. You could negotiate a better price on just about anything these days; whitegoods, furniture, anything. And accordingly, Quentin was usually happy to knock ten per cent off the marked price if it would secure a sale. But right now he wasn't feeling overly generous. The heat and the pain were making him irritable, impatient. Besides which—

Quentin clasped the dangling ticket between his thumb and forefinger, and indicated a second figure—smaller, with a red line through it—printed slightly above the first.

"Honestly, I'd love to," he lied, "but we've got a sale on. There's the original price. Already discounted from two-fifty. One ninety-nine's the best I can do."

The customer gave Quentin a look, actually making eye-contact. "Come on—I *know* you can do better on the price."

Quentin's smile thinned. "No, sorry, I really can't." He shrugged regretfully. "One-ninety-nine's the final price."

"Better price for cash?"

"No." Quentin folded his arms across his chest and glanced at the clock again. 5.25 pm. *Bloody hell! How can the time be passing so quickly? And me stuck with a haggler!* "I can throw in the light bulb, but that's it."

The customer stared at Quentin for a moment. Then a small, arrogant smile touched the corner of his mouth, his expression becoming one of amused scepticism.

Quentin felt a sudden flash of rage and resentment, followed immediately by a agonised spasming in his stomach. Sweat dripped from his forehead into his eyes, and he blinked fiercely, unwilling to break eye-contact with the customer. He gritted his teeth. "It's a good price—genuine sale price, genuine discount."

The customer raised an eyebrow. "Bronte Lighting always do better on their prices."

"Bronte Lighting," said Quentin, coldly, "have a bigger mark-up. They can *afford* to knock their prices down!" *Stop it!* He pressed a hand to his stomach. *Never rubbish the competition; it makes you look bitter and desperate.* He took a deep breath, and smiled as politely as he could. "We don't mark our goods up so much, so our prices are still better than most other stores can offer. Even *with* a discount." *Nice. Informative without being pushy. Now for the clincher.* "But you needn't take my word for it—shop around, compare prices. I can pretty-much guarantee you won't find a better deal elsewhere."

The customer pursed his lips and regarded the fitting again, a thoughtful expression on his face.

Got you! Taking advantage of the customer's distraction, Quentin surreptitiously wiped the sweat from his brow with the back of his hand. *So hot. But I'm back in control.* The pain in his stomach began to ease. *That's it, take it easy. Not worth stressing over. All turns out okay if you exercise a little control—*

"Trade price?"

Quentin blinked. "Sorry?"

"What's the trade price on this fitting?" asked the customer, annunciating carefully, as if speaking to a rather stupid child.

The muscles in Quentin's neck tightened. His stomach began to cramp, pushing the burning sensation further up throat. Swallowing, he regarded the customer's formal attire pointedly. "You're a tradesman?"

"You *can* do better for trade?"

"On presentation of a tradesman's card, yes."

"So—you *can* do further discounts, then." Again, that small, arrogant smile.

Quentin was beginning to feel really unwell. In addition to the pain in his abdomen, there was a disturbing tightness in his chest. He glanced at the clock again. 5.40 pm. *Surely not!* "For tradesmen, yes. Are you a tradesman?"

The customer looked down his nose at Quentin. "Does it *matter?*"

"Tradesmen get a better discount because they generally buy in bulk."

The customer regarded Quentin blankly.

Quentin licked his lips. "Look—if we sell in bulk, we can re-order in bulk, which means we can negotiate a better price with our suppliers. Which in turn means that selling at a trade price—to tradesmen— doesn't hurt our bottom line."

Another pause.

Quentin cleared his throat. "Of course, we *can* do trade prices for bulk *retail* purchases…"

"So—" the customer regarded the pendant again, "—if I were to buy ten of these…?"

Quentin beamed genuinely. "Well, for ten, I could knock a further ten per cent off the sale price. That'd bring it down to trade." He paused. "I'm pretty sure I've got ten in stock right now, if you're interested—"

"Can you do the same price for one?"

Quentin stared unbelievingly. "No," he said, carefully. "As I've just explained, we can only do trade on a bulk purchase. Sale price is the best we can do on a single item."

The customer sniffed. "How about for cash?"

A buzzing sound seemed to fill Quentin's head. Sweat began to drip freely from his forehead, and the shop blurred around him. His stomach cramped violently, forcing hot bile into the back of his throat. "The price," he heard himself saying, as if from a great distance, "for one of these pendants, is *one-hundred and ninety-nine dollars.* I'll give you a moment to decide."

He stumbled away, back behind the counter, leaning heavily against the counter-top. The cool Formica surface chilled his stomach through his sweat-soaked shirt. *Relief!* Trembling, he fumbled at his collar, loosening his tie. *Calm down!* He swallowed heavily, but the pain in his chest refused to subside. *Grab some antacid on the way home.* Quentin raised his head and stared blearily at the clock. 6.00 pm. *Something has to be wrong with that bloody thing!* He swallowed again, wiped his forehead with shaking hands, and straightened up. *Relax. Close the sale. Shut up shop. Go home*

He lowered his gaze and found himself face-to-face with the customer, standing on the opposite side of the counter. He flinched. "Er…have you decided yet?"

"Forget about the hanging lights," the customer made a dismissive gesture. "I'll get them cheaper elsewhere."

"Fair enough," said Quentin, coldly. He glanced pointedly at the clock. "Well, if that's all—"

"Do you stock light bulbs?"

"What?" *Getting hard to breathe—heartburn or heat?*

"Light bulbs. Got any light bulbs?"

Quentin slowly turned to stare at the set of shelves dominating the wall behind him, packed from floor to ceiling with every variety of light bulb imaginable, all boxed either individually or shrink-wrapped in packs of ten. Quentin regarded the display for a moment, then turned back to the customer. "Of *course* we have light bulbs!" he snapped. "This is a *light* shop!"

"Hmph. So you have light bulbs, then?"

"*Yes!*" Quentin hissed, pressing his sweating palms hard against the counter-top.

"Well. I need some light bulbs."

Quentin gritted his teeth. "What sort of bulb?"

"The sort you twist in."

"Ah." Quentin nodded curtly, drops of perspiration falling from the tip of his nose. "Edison Screw." He stepped towards the appropriate shelf.

"No, no, *no!*" the customer snapped. "The *twist*-in sort!"

Quentin balled his hands into tight, moist fists. "Edison Screw *is* the twist-in sort." He plucked a sample from the shelf, turned, and thrust it under the customer's nose. "*See?*"

A look of triumph spread across the customer's face. "This is a *screw-in* globe."

Quentin narrowed his eyes, not trusting himself to ask the obvious question.

"I asked for a *twist-in* globe." The customer made a twisting motion with his hand. "The sort with the two pins on the base. Twist-in. Not with a screw."

Comprehension dawned, and with it came a sense of deep relief. *Almost done!* "You mean a *Bayonet Cap*. A clip-in."

The customer shrugged irritably. "Twist-in, clip-in, what's the difference?"

Pain. Heat. Quentin opened his mouth to retort, then closed it again. What was the point? He nodded tiredly.

"Fine. Bayonet caps. What wattage were you after?"

"One hundred watts."

Quentin nodded, and reached for the requested item.

"Is that okay to put into a small table lamp?"

Quentin froze, refusing to turn around. "No. The biggest wattage you should be using is forty watts."

"How about seventy-five?"

"No," said Quentin, as patiently as he could. "Forty."

"Sixty?"

"*No!*"

"So you reckon forty, do you?"

"*Yes!*"

"*Weeeeeeeeeeeeeeeeell*…okay, then."

"*Fine!*" snapped Quentin. "Pearl or clear?"

"Which gives better light?"

"Well, clear gives a more *direct* light—"

"Fine."

Quentin reached for a pack of clear globes.

"I'll take the pearl."

Quentin hunched forward slightly as cramps gripped his entire chest. "Pearl?"

The customer took a moment to consider. "Yes. Yes, pearl, I think."

Quentin nodded curtly, and took a pack of pearl globes from the shelf.

"No, actually, make that clear."

Quentin thrust the pack roughly back onto the shelf, grabbed a pack of clear bulbs, spun around and slammed it down on the counter. Something inside the pack tinkled ominously.

The customer eyed the pack dubiously. "I think you broke one."

"They're fine!" Quentin snapped. "How many did you want?"

The customer pursed his lips. "How much per bulb?"

"One dollar."

"Hm. Well then, I'll taaaaaaaaaaaaaaaaaaaaaaaaaaaaaaake—" the customer drew the word out for a full ten seconds as he considered the dilemma at hand.

Quentin bit his lip. It was really getting hard to breathe. *So hot!* "Yes??" he prompted, choking down the bile rising in his gullet.

The customer blinked, regarding the pack in front of him. "Hm…"

Quentin waited, every muscle tensed.

The customer opened his mouth to speak, appeared to reconsider, closed it again, then gave a satisfied nod, obviously having come to a decision. "Do I get a better price if I buy the whole pack?"

Quentin stared at him.

"How about if I pay cash?"

"*NO!*" screamed Quentin. "*NO BETTER PRICE FOR CASH! THE PRICE IS ONE DOLLAR PER BULB! ONE MISERABLE DOLLAR! I DON'T CARE WHETHER YOU PAY BY CASH, CHEQUE, CREDIT CARD OR BLOODY BEADS! I DON'T CARE WHETHER YOU BUY*

ONE BULB OR TWENTY THOUSAND BLOODY BULBS—THE PRICE IS, AND ALWAYS WILL BE, ONE—GODDAMNED—DOL—"

He stopped abruptly, eyes bulging, as a burning vice seemed to crush his heart. Gasping, he clutched at his chest.

Can't breathe!

Crimson-faced, he sprawled against the counter, his entire body slicked with sweat.

Heartburn, my arse! I'm having a fucking heart attack!

His mind fogged by pain and heat, Quentin suddenly became aware that he was being addressed.

"…never been spoken to in such a way in all my life!" the customer was saying, apparently oblivious to Quentin's plight. "It's simply outrageous! I don't know how you expect to stay in business with an attitude like yours, but I can assure you that nobody *I* know will ever frequent *this* establishment!"

In a burst of rage, Quentin lunged at the customer. Then his chest seemed to explode, and he fell backwards to the floor. Panic-stricken, he stared up at the customer's head, just visible over the edge of the counter. "*Please... Help...*"

The customer didn't move, ceiling lights silhouetting his head, hiding his face in darkness. "You know what your problem is? Anger."

Quentin blinked, and the shop seemed to *waver*, shimmering as though a furnace door had been flung open nearby. *Must breathe!* But his lungs refused to obey, sitting like lead weights in his chest, pinning him to the floor.

Unbelievably the customer *grinned*, perfect white teeth shining from the black hole of his face. "Dangerous thing, repression of anger. Causes all sorts of problems, mental *and* physical. Aneurysms, strokes, heart attacks—but I guess I don't need to tell you that, do I?"

Quentin's vision began to dim. There was a ferocious roaring sound in his ears. He blinked again. The roaring grew louder.

Then flames seemed to burst through the walls, thick black smoke filling the air. Light fittings warped and melted, glass cracking in the heat. The Gyprock panels on the ceiling caught fire, crumbling to expose nests of electrical wiring which immediately began to melt and char. A crimson haze filtered through the shop.

The squeal of burning plastic sounded like screaming.

Hallucinating.

Then the flames reached him.

Quentin writhed in agony, as every square centimetre of his exposed skin began to crackle and peel.

And suddenly he *remembered*.

"And always just too late," said the customer, as if reading Quentin's mind. Miraculously untouched by the surrounding inferno, he stepped casually around the counter and squatted down beside Quentin. "Don't worry. We've got an eternity to work on your problem. Maybe one day you'll remember *before* the anger gets out of control."

He stood up, and gave Quentin a final grin.

"Same time tomorrow, then, eh? As usual."

And then there was only heat and pain.

What Goes Uptime

As soon as the gunfire begins, I'm sprinting for the lift. One advantage of all that procedural crap the military drums into us techs: you don't waste time thinking when the crunch comes. *Get to the Platform and burn the hardware before it falls into Coalition hands.*

The lift doors close behind me. The lights flicker, then go out, plunging the interior into blackness. I smack the emergency button, but power *and* backup have gone. How is that possible? I jam my fingers between the lift doors, trying to force them apart.

The sound of gunfire and screaming and running feet pours in from outside, and I step back from the doors. I don't recognise the sound of the gun. Not Coalition, unless it's something new. Odd. Coalition prefer old tech. And how the hell did they breach security without tripping the alarm?

Maybe we should have listened to McKay. A loon, to be sure, but he certainly knows his jumptech. One of his recent gripes is that if Coalition forces developed their *own* hardware, they could ambush a hunting party downtime and ride *our* Platform back into the complex. Guess he was right.

It's gone very quiet outside. Either Security's dealt with the hostiles, or—

I'm still thinking about the sound of that gun, though. And then I remember another of McKay's nasty little theories:

In a nutshell, you can do what you like in the past without affecting established history. Set off a nuke in ancient Rome, and the nuked-Rome timeline branches off as an alternate reality, while we can still jump back to 'our' reality because spacetime 'recognises' us as a product of that specific timeline. That's why Top Brass makes the Platform available to the occasional private hunting party. Bag yourself a T-rex. Or a President. All good, clean, *safe* fun.

But what happens (asks McKay) if you keep encouraging the attitude that you can run amok in the past without consequence? What if the Platform continues to exist up to a point in the future where standard moral values have evolved directly from those our backjumpers are adopting *now*?

I scream as the lift doors burst inward, metal peeling back like paper as something huge and humanoid—silhouetted against the neon glare of the corridor—punches its way in. Sharp teeth gleam whitely against the darkness. Its right paw grips an object resembling an oversized Uzi; its left clasps an enormous, bladed weapon.

Hanging from a belt around its middle is a freshly severed human head. It's McKay, ginning at me as if to say: *Told ya!*

Smug bastard.

Hunting party's here.

The Shadow Over Bexley

Later, Eric would berate himself for not just sodding off home as soon as Ted mentioned the words 'motivational tour'…

"New bloke coming along tonight." Ted sipped at his shandy, leaning casually on his walking-frame.

Mike raised a greying eyebrow. "Didn't know we had an initiation scheduled."

Eric frowned. "Shouldn't be discussing Lodge business in public!" he grouched into his beer. Unconsciously, his free hand wandered to the Sacred Insignia sewn over the breast of his crimson robes. "It's bloody disrespectful!"

Ted looked pained. "We're in the Lodge *bar*. Anyway," he said to Mike, "he's not a recruit. Some big-wig from an affiliated order overseas."

"Bloody Yank!" muttered Eric. "Bet he's a bloody Yank! Met enough bloody Yanks in Korea to last me a bloody lifetime! Bloody Yanks!"

"New England, apparently."

"That's off the coast of Scotland, isn't it?" asked Mike.

"Nah, that's the Falklands. New England's in America."

"Bloody Yanks!" Eric scratched savagely at his chin with an arthritic, liver-spotted hand. *Bastards think they own the world, and now they're poking their noses into our bloody Lodge!*

"Anyway," Ted continued, "this bloke just turns up on Ken's doorstep, here on a 'motivational tour'. At least, that's what Steve told me. And he heard it from Fred, who heard it from Bert. And Bert heard it from Kevin, who was there when this bloke arrived."

"What the hell's a motivational tour?" demanded Eric.

"Pep talks. Wants to get us enthused about the sacred rituals again."

Eric sniffed dismissively. Admittedly, the fortnightly meetings had lacked a certain something of late. Oh, the sacred rituals of The Order of the Mottled Gecko (Bexley) were all still properly observed, as they had been since the Order's inception in 1949; the secret handshake (thumbs in), the naming of The Artefacts (The Letter Opener and The Glass Eye, donated by the late Arthur Nonce), and, of course, the chook raffle afterwards. But the sense of purpose once associated with these rituals had waned. Eric suspected that, like himself—though he'd never have admitted it—many of the members were beginning to feel that the idea of a bunch of senior citizens running around in robes was…well, a bit silly.

Still, it was one thing to *think* such things, quite another to actually suggest that they needed to drag in some bloody Yank motivational speaker! Besides which, there was a certain comfort in the predictability of the meetings, and Eric wasn't sure he could be bothered getting all enthused about the rituals again.

The thin bingling of the gong drifted through the bar.

"Here we go," said Ted, draining his shandy. "All in, fellas."

They trudged dutifully into the main hall to join the other forty or so attendees, a collective shuffling filling the oak-beamed building as they bumbled about between the fold-down modular pews, exchanging mumbled greetings through ill-fitting dentures, seeking their usual seats.

Barely had they sat down when the gong bingled again, and they struggled back to their feet, rheumy eyes cast reverently floorward.

With a flourish of purple robes, the Illustrious Potentate (Ken McGinnis, from No. 42) took the rostrum at the front of the hall, adjusting the microphone carefully. There was a squeal of feedback, and those with hearing-aids grimaced. The Illustrious Potentate cleared his throat. "We thank The Almighty for His protection and guidance, and pledge faithfully to serve Him, and to uphold the sanctity and secrecy of Our Order."

"Mumble-umble-umble," echoed the congregation.

The Illustrious Potentate bowed his head momentarily, then sighed, fished his spectacles out from under his robes, put them on, and beamed at the congregation. "Well, welcome along once again," he said, as the assemblage resumed their seats. "We'll be getting to the usual Lodge business in just a moment, but first I'd like to begin with something a little different." He paused to let the enormity of this statement sink in.

The congregation looked appropriately awed. And well they might, thought Eric. There hadn't been a change in the running-order of the Lodge meetings since…well, ever. Not unless you counted the time Neddy Johnston had his conniption fit during the Rite of the Ascendant Hairpiece…

"Gentlemen," Ken continued, "it gives me very great pleasure to introduce our guest speaker for tonight. Will you please welcome, from our affiliated Arkham Lodge, The Esoteric Order of Dagon—"

"What'd he say?" Mike whispered to Ted. "Ethnic Order of the Dago?"

"—the Most High Seer, Jebediah Marsh," concluded Ken, and there was a patter of polite applause as he took a seat in the front-row pew.

There was a pause, then a man emerged from the shadows behind the rostrum; tall, lean, and dressed in a snappy black suit. Stepping up to the microphone, he gazed at the congregation for a moment with dark, piercing eyes, his pallid face utterly devoid of expression. The effect, thought Eric, was quite unsettling. *Not bad enough he's a Yank, but a creepy Yank to boot!*

The congregation shuffled. Somebody coughed pointedly.

Marsh blinked, then grinned; a brilliant toothy smile that instantly transformed his face from ghoulish to simply manic. "Hey, thanks guys! Great to be here!" His powerful voice filled the hall. "How you all doing tonight?"

Silence.

"C'mon, guys!" he prompted. "Let's hear it—*how you feeling tonight?* Good? Yeah? C'mon let's hear it!"

There was a half-hearted muttering from the congregation.

"Great! Okay!" Marsh clapped his hands together theatrically, and the congregation started. "I wanna kick off by asking you all a real important question." He paused, eyeing his audience speculatively. "Why do you do it?"

The members of the congregation glanced sidelong at one-another.

"I mean, hey," Marsh spread his hands wide, "the public service, the charity work—why do you actually *do* it?"

Silence.

"Anyone?"

Ted hesitantly raised his hand.

Marsh pointed. "Yeah! What's your name?"

"Um…Ted."

"Okay Ted, stand up so we can all hear you! Big hand for Ted, everyone!" Ted clambered stiffly to his feet, as Marsh led the bemused congregation in a round of applause. "Okay, Ted—why do we do the charity work?"

"Because…it gives us a sense of satisfaction?"

Marsh nodded thoughtfully. "Yeah, not bad, but *why* does it give us a sense of satisfaction?" He glanced around the hall again as Ted sat down. "Let me tell you what *I* think, okay?" He paused for a moment, steepling his fingers. "I believe we find the community work satisfying because it makes us feel superior to those we're assisting. Makes us feel important—*powerful*, even."

The congregation began to mutter rebelliously. *What a load of crap!* thought Eric.

"So we all agree," Marsh continued. "We do it for the power. Problem is, community service doesn't really give you power. Not real life-and-death-over-others power, which—let's face it—is the only kinda power that really matters. So—" his eyes gleamed, "—how do we go about *achieving* that power?"

Silence.

"Okay, here's an easier question—what sets a Lodge apart from other community groups? What do we do that's different? Anyone?"

Mike raised his hand.

"Yes! What's your name? Mike? Let's hear it for Mike, everyone! Okay, Mike—what's the answer?"

"The rituals?"

"Yes! The rituals, exactly! And why do we go through the rituals? Anyone?"

There was a very long pause. Marsh obviously wasn't going to answer this one for them, Eric realised, but the rest of the silly old buggers hadn't twigged yet. The silence continued. Eventually, Eric could stand it no longer. "Tradition!" he snapped.

Piercing eyes met Eric's own, and Eric felt a chill run down his spine. He'd never been given to flights of wild fancy, but Marsh's gaze—well, it was like looking into the eyes of a fish. Cold orbs, untouched by the manic grin. Almost as if Marsh's body was nothing but a fleshy puppet, outwardly expressing an emotion that went unfelt by the inhuman puppeteer within.

"Yes! What's your name?" asked Marsh.

Eric hesitated, prompting several of his peers to turn around in their seats and squint expectantly at him. "Eric," he said, grudgingly.

Marsh grinned. "Well, Eric, you're absolutely right! Performance of the rituals is a tradition—" he eyed the congregation again, "—*and nothing more!* It doesn't actually serve any useful purpose." He paused. "Am I right?"

Silence. Then, a mutter of reluctant agreement.

Bastard! thought Eric hatefully. *Why not just come out and say it? That none of it means anything. That we're just a bunch of pathetic old farts pottering about in a stupid little club! Motivational speaker, my arse!*

"So," Marsh continued, eyes narrowing conspiratorially, "wouldn't it be great if the rituals contributed *directly* to your accumulation of power?"

There was a pause, as the congregation digested this notion.

"Okay, listen, let's get everyone standing up!" Marsh beamed enthusiastically. "C'mon, everyone up!" There was a reluctant shuffling as the gathering rose. "Great stuff, that's it! Now, I want each of you to grab the hand of the person either side of you, form a chain across each row…"

"Bugger that!" muttered Eric, loudly.

Marsh smiled sympathetically. "Hey, that's okay. If you're not comfortable with this, just sit back and join in whenever you're ready." He glanced around. "Okay, what I'm gonna do now is teach you all a chant we use in Arkham—nothing complicated, just a little something to clear and focus the mind."

Good luck with this lot, thought Eric, sourly. *Most of 'em can't remember what they had for lunch.*

"Okay, repeat after me." Marsh raised his arms dramatically above his head. *"Iä! Iä! Cthulhu fhtagn!"*

Hesitantly, the congregation repeated the phrase, aging tongues grappling with the unfamiliar syllables.

"Again!" Marsh commanded, and they grudgingly obeyed. "And again!"

The words were beginning to flow more smoothly.

"And again—keep it going! *Iä! Iä! Cthulhu fhtagn! Iä! Iä! Cthulhu fhtagn!"*

Eric looked around incredulously at his fellow members; bright-eyed, chanting along with the sort of enthusiasm usually reserved for an RSL buffet. *What the hell's gotten into them? It's as if they're actually getting off on this…gibberish!*

And yet…

Eric blinked. There *was* a rather pleasant rhythm to the words, comforting yet invigorating. Made him feel secure. *Powerful.* As though he could do anything… Slowly, his senses began to dull, the chant reverberating in his head. Reality faded—

A sudden squeal of feedback tore through the veil of sleep, the entire congregation starting as Marsh tapped the microphone sharply. *Jesus!* thought Eric. *What's he trying to do—give us all heart attacks?* Which, he reflected, was a distinct risk with this crowd.

"Hey, that was great!" Marsh beamed. "Give yourselves a big hand! C'mon! You did a great job! Yeah, c'mon!" A patter of applause started up, slowly swelling to a roar as the congregation enthusiastically demonstrated their appreciation. Marsh nodded his thanks. "Hey, listen, you guys have been really great, but I'm afraid my time's up for tonight—"

Eric glanced at his watch. A full hour had passed!

"—so I'll let you get back to the usual Lodge business, and just say thanks a whole bunch for having me, and I'll be back next week to show you the next step in the Real Power Program! Have a great night!" He waved cheerily, stepping back from the rostrum as Ken rose from his seat and added a few words of thanks.

Ted nudged Eric. "Can't wait to see what happens next meeting, eh?"

Eric snorted. "Count me out! Never heard so much blasphemous crap in all my life!" The activities of the Lodge were firmly grounded in the Christian faith, and there had seemed to Eric to be a distinctly un-Christian feel to that chant. Not that Eric was particularly devout, or anything. Not even a Sunday Christian, really. But—well, dammit, it was just *wrong,* that was all!

And yet, he had to admit, there *had* been some sort of power behind that chant. And he wasn't altogether sure that he didn't want to feel that sense of power again…

Eric chewed his lip. It couldn't hurt to attend the next meeting, he decided, just to see what happened.

"Should be a good one tonight!" said Ted, sipping his shandy.

Mike nodded agreement. Eric shrugged listlessly. He'd been unable to think of anything but that damned chant all week, and despite wanting to hear it again, to feel the accompanying sense of power, he still couldn't shake the feeling that there was something wrong about all of this. Something he couldn't quite put his finger on.

Creepy Yank.

Eric nodded. Ah, yes. *That* was it.

The gong bingled.

"All in, fellas," said Ted.

The hall had undergone some changes since the last meeting. Black bedsheets hung from the walls, shrouding the floor at the front of the hall, giving it the cheesy appearance of a witches' grotto at a high-school fête. In place of the rostrum sat—well, the only word Eric could think of was 'eyesore'. The thing was clearly supposed to be an altar of some sort, although it looked more like a chest-high pile of rubble; fist-sized lumps of black rock (or paper mâché, more likely) piled haphazardly together, with a thick slab of stone (Styrofoam?) lying atop it.

Eric sniffed contemptuously, and took his seat.

A few moments later a figure emerged from the shadows behind the altar, and the congregation fell silent. Dressed in a long black cloak, Marsh approached the altar, bowed his head for a moment, then looked up and grinned. "Hey, how you all doing tonight? Great to see you all back again! Tonight we're going to pick up where we left off last time––you all remember the chant? Okay, great, well, let's get everyone up the front here and we can get started!"

The congregation obligingly shuffled from their seats up to the front of the hall, where they stood milling around, waiting for further direction.

"Okay, I want everyone to form a circle around myself and the altar. That's it, big circle. Now," Marsh continued, "before we start, I want to explain a little bit about tonight's ritual, and how it fits in with our plans."

So stop waffling, and bloody get on with it! thought Eric.

Impossibly, as if he'd read his mind, Marsh shot Eric a look. Eric shuddered.

Marsh grinned again. "Okay, the thing to remember is that The Esoteric Order of Dagon, like most Lodges, is essentially a Christian organisation." Again, he glanced at Eric. "I know some of you may have had concerns in that regard, but there's nothing sinister about the rituals we use. Like you guys, the EOD takes certain specific aspects of Christianity, which we modify to better suit our particular requirements. Of course, most of these changes are just cosmetic— f'rinstance, we don't refer to 'God', but to 'Dagon', although we're basically talking about the same guy, okay?"

Eric rolled his eyes. A few other members of the congregation looked doubtful, but the rest nodded agreeably. This was something they could relate to, thought Eric sourly; the theatrical aspect of the Lodge, which made an otherwise fairly dull set of activities a bit more exciting.

"Now," Marsh continued, "one of the EOD's cornerstone beliefs is that Dagon can actually be induced to intervene *directly* in mortal affairs—y'know, put in the occasional appearance, spread around a little of that godly power." This raised a chuckle from the congregation. "I mean, hey, why worship a God who only rewards his followers after they die?"

Christianity, my eye! thought Eric. *This is bloody pagan worship! Can't these stupid old buggers see that?* He opened his mouth to speak his mind, but was silenced by another bone-chilling look from Marsh.

"Problem is," Marsh went on, "Dagon lives in a whole other dimension from ours. So, if we want to share in his power—which we do, right?" There was a chorus of agreement. "Well, it's up to us to open a dimensional portal which he can use to get here!"

The congregation nodded eagerly, hanging on his every word. *What the hell's wrong with them?* Eric wondered. *It's as if he's got some sort of hold over them! Little creep'll be advocating human sacrifice in a moment!*

"Now, the great thing about this program," said Marsh, "is that it doesn't take a lifetime, just three simple steps. Firstly," he held up a finger, "we have to draw Dagon's attention to this exact point in time and space, which we did last week with the chanting. Secondly," he held up another finger, "we need to give him a reason to *remember* this location. And that's what we'll be doing tonight!" He turned, gesturing off to his right. "Guys, you all know Mike—well, Mike's going to be helping me out with tonight's ritual, so let's give him a big hand! C'mon up here, Mike!" Beaming, Mike bumbled up to Marsh, shaking his hand warmly as the congregation applauded. "Up onto the altar, thanks Mike. Lying down." Marsh addressed the congregation again as Mike complied. "Okay guys, what I need you to do is hold hands, forming an unbroken chain around the altar, and then I want you to start chanting again. Everyone remember the chant? *Iä! Iä! Cthulhu fhtagn!* Okay?"

There was a babble of assent. Eric glanced around the circle. The faces of his peers shone with enthusiasm. *More exciting than rolling Arthur Nonce's glass eye across a Ouija board, I s'pose,* he thought grudgingly. *But still, it's just another bloody ritual. Why so enthused?* He eyed Marsh suspiciously. *He's definitely got a hold over them. Lucky I'm made of sterner stuff...*

"Oh, and just one more thing," Marsh added, an uncharacteristically serious expression on his face. "Whatever you see and hear during the ritual, don't—under *any* circumstances—break the circle! And keep the chant going until—" he paused, and a sly smile touched the corners of his mouth, "—well, you'll know when to stop, believe me! So, let's hear it—*Iä! Iä! Cthulhu fhtagn! Iä! Iä! Cthulhu fhtagn!*"

The congregation took up the chant with gusto, their voices filling the hall. Again, Eric experienced that odd sensation of comfort and power. Realising he was the only person not chanting, he began mouthing the words, glancing surreptitiously about him. Marsh didn't seem to be chanting in sync with the others. Eric strained his ears, and caught part of Marsh's incantation; *"Iä! Dagon! Iä! Cthulhu! Ngai ygnaiih! Iä! Iä! Cthulhu fhtagn! Iä! Iä! Dagon!"*

Marsh's chanting grew louder, the congregation increasing their volume to match his.

A weird green glow began to emanate from the altar, shining dimly between the rocks.

"Iä! Iä! Cthulhu fhtagn! Iä! Iä! Cthulhu fhtagn!"

Marsh reached beneath his cloak and withdrew a long, ceremonial-looking dagger from his belt, holding it aloft with both hands.

"Iä! Dagon! Nyah ph'naii! Gi! Gi! Dagon! Dagon! DAGON!"

With a horrifying flash of clarity, Eric realised what was about to happen. He opened his mouth to shout a warning—

And Marsh slammed the dagger down.

Mike let out a single, piercing shriek, his hands jerking like poisoned spiders. Then he slumped motionless, eyes staring.

The chanting stopped.

"Hold the circle!" Marsh commanded. He carefully withdrew the dagger, wiping both sides of the blade clean against Mike's robes.

Somebody began to mutter nervously. Eric gagged. *Maniac! He's just killed Mike!*

A hideous sucking noise arose from the altar. The congregation stared as Mike began to twitch and jerk. The sucking became a loathsome gobbling, as a pig might make at a feeding trough. Imperceptibly at first, then with increasing speed, Mike began to sink *into* the altar-top like a hot knife into butter. Hands and feet vanished. Knees and elbows. Torso. A cloud of vapour shrouded the altar, a sickly-sweet odour filling the air—

The vapour cleared. Mike was gone, the altar vacant. No glow, just an unremarkable pile of stones.

Silence.

Marsh took a step back, tucked the dagger away beneath his cloak, and bowed his head. Then he straightened, glanced around, and grinned. "Hey, fantastic job, guys! Give yourselves a big hand—and let's hear it for my partner in crime, Mike!"

There was a brief, uncomprehending silence.

Then someone chuckled.

Someone else began to applaud.

In moments, the entire congregation was clapping and laughing and cheering appreciatively.

Marsh beamed.

"Oh, I don't believe it!" Ted grinned incredulously. "It was all a bloody illusion!"

"Who—what?" Eric stammered.

"A magic trick! Bloody convincing, too!"

"Trick?" Eric gazed at the altar.

"And Mike was in on it!" Ted shook his head wonderingly. "He's a bloody dark horse, isn't he? Boring as batshit, usually. I s'pose after we've gone home tonight, Marsh'll open the top of that altar, Mike'll climb out, and they'll both have a bloody good laugh at our expense!"

Eric didn't trust himself to answer…

Mike was conspicuous by his absence at the next meeting.

Eric and Ted stood silently in the bar; Ted drinking, Eric regarding Ted hatefully over the rim of his glass. He'd spent the past week dreading this meeting, dreading the prospect of turning up and finding his suspicions confirmed. Mike had been murdered; of that, Eric was certain. Well, almost certain. He'd been nursing a tiny shred of hope that it *had* been a trick. But now…

"Odd, isn't it?" he remarked bitterly. "Mike not being here this week."

Ted shrugged. Eric glared at him. *Don't you care?* he felt like screaming. *Don't you understand what's happened?* Marsh's influence over the congregation had grown; that was obvious. *So it's up to me,* he thought. *It's up to me to—*

—To do what? Call the police? Eric cringed. He'd already tried that. Sort of. That is, he'd picked up the phone, the morning after the last meeting, and begun dialling 000. And then he'd stopped. What if it *had* been a trick? He'd look a right bloody fool if he went and reported a non-existent murder. And even if Mike had been murdered, what the hell could Eric say to the cops? *Yes officer, I'd like to report a murder. A friend of mine's been sacrificed by a mad pagan cultist at a Masonic*

Lodge meeting. The body? Oh, sucked into another dimension and consumed by some eldritch god, apparently...

They'd put him away. Better to wait, just in case Mike did turn up…

The gong bingled. Ted drained his shandy. "All in, fellas."

The hall was still set up as it had been last meeting, and Marsh beckoned them all up to the altar. "Hey guys! How you all doing? Great to see you! Okay, let's get everyone into a circle around the altar, and we can get started—"

"Where's Mike?" Eric demanded. "How come he's not here?"

His peers frowned disapprovingly at the outburst. Marsh regarded Eric carefully. "Who knows? Having a quiet night in?" He held Eric's gaze for a moment, then returned his attention to the general congregation. "Anyway, tonight we should see the fruit of all your hard work over the past few meetings—and hey, give yourselves a big hand, you've really earned it!"

There was a burst of tumultuous applause.

"Now," said Marsh, as the applause died down, "I want you to understand that there are risks involved in tonight's ritual. But if we stick to the program, it'll all be worth it. At our first meeting we drew the attention of the Elder Gods to this location with our chanting. At the next meeting we gave them an incentive to stick around, waiting for the doorway to open again—blood sacrifice." He met Eric's gaze again. "Of course, we can't actually go around sacrificing our members—" the congregation chuckled appreciatively, "—but even a mock-sacrifice, with the promise of bloodshed to come, should get Dagon's attention. And tonight we're going to take advantage of that and draw him in. Except he won't find any blood when he arrives—just a containment spell, which'll hold him in our dimension while protecting us from him. And then we'll be in a position to demand anything we want!" Marsh's eyes shone maniacally, his expression mirrored in the faces of the congregation. "So, let's start by holding hands and getting that chant going! *Iä! Iä! Cthulhu fhtagn! Iä! Iä! Cthulhu fhtagn!*"

Mock-sacrifice, my arse! thought Eric. *Poor Mike isn't at home— he was murdered to satisfy this maniac's lust for power! I'm getting the hell out of here!* He tried to step forward, but strong hands either side of him held him firm. *"Ted! Please! Let go!"* he hissed.

Ted ignored the plea, spittle spraying from his dentures as he continued to chant, eyes shining feverishly. *"Iä! Iä! Cthulhu fhtagn! Iä! Iä! Cthulhu fhtagn!"*

The floorboards seemed to throb beneath Eric's feet as the chanting grew steadily louder. His head swam, and the altar again began to glow like some fetid night-blooming fungus.

"IÄ! IÄ! CTHULHU FHTAGN! IÄ! IÄ! CTHULHU FHTAGN!"

"IÄ! DAGON!" bellowed Marsh. *"IÄ! CTHULHU! IÄ! NYARLATHOTEP Ë YOG-SOTHOTH! N'YAH MGAWAH'AL N'GAII Ë DAGON!"*

The space above the altar *shimmered* as if in the grip of a heatwave, and suddenly there was a hole, dark and apparently bottomless, the mouth of which floated mid-air in blatant defiance of the laws of physics.

"IÄ! IÄ! CTHULHU FHTAGN!"

Gaping, Eric stared into the blackness.

Something terrible stared back at him.

Eric screamed, his mind filtering the image in an effort to preserve his sanity. *Huge. Hungry eyes. Coiled limbs. Rubbery. Gelid. Monstrous claws. Reaching out—*

"DAGON!" bellowed Marsh. *"BUGG-SHOGGOG Y'HAH Y'HA-NTHLEI—!"*

"NO!" screamed Eric. Breaking free of the circle, he threw himself at Marsh, ignoring the pain in his arthritic limbs. *"IT'S COMING THROUGH! YOU'LL KILL US ALL!"*

Caught off-guard, Marsh stopped mid-chant as Eric fell against him. "What the hell—?" Abruptly, his expression changed to one of utter terror. *"THE CONTAINMENT SPELL!"* he shrieked. *"I HAVEN'T COMPLETED—!"*

Quick as lightning, vast talons reached from the hole, engulfed Marsh, and withdrew.

Silence.

Torn from their hypnotic state, the congregation stared in horror. Choking with fear, rooted to the spot, Eric stared into the darkness. He blinked—

And something rushed towards him.

He shrieked, turning to flee, and an agonising pressure enfolded his body, squeezing the breath from his lungs. *Heart attack?*

Dragged backwards into the darkness at freight-train speed, he felt himself raised up impossibly high. A vast chasm opened before him. *Purple. Moist. Lined with endless rows of white, pointed—*

—teeth?

Should have just sodded off home the moment Ted mentioned the words 'motivational tour', was Eric's last thought.

The Second-Hand Bookshop of Al Hazred

"Rover! Geddown!"

Releasing the customer's leg, the shoggoth burbled sheepishly back to its basket next to the door. Al smiled an apology, sighing inwardly as he noted the intricately carved Tsathogguan casket the customer was carrying. *Selling, not buying.* "Sorry about that. How can I help you?"

The customer plonked the casket down on the counter. "Um…I've got some books I'm wanting to sell?" He glanced around the darkened interior of the shop, at the haphazard maze of rickety, floor-to-ceiling bookcases stacked with countless piles of yellowing tomes. His expression—one all-too-familiar to Al—was of thinly veiled contempt. "Wondered if you might be interested." He leant against the counter, then recoiled, brushing dust from his elbows.

Al nodded wearily. *Think I don't know the bloody place is a shambles? The Old Ones' benevolence doesn't extend to new shop-fittings. If I could just scrape together enough to get a wood-whisperer on to regenerating the shelves…* "Well, let's see what you've got…" He began to pick his way through the contents of the casket, taking the books out one-by-one and stacking them on the counter. "*The Book of Eibon*…"

"Very collectible, I believe."

Al examined the inside cover and shook his head. "Twelfth edition. Ten-a-penny. What else have we got here? *Revelations of Glaaki, The Ponape Scriptures, Unaussprechlichen Kulten*—all Readers' Digest editions. Hmm…*Cthâat Aquadingen*—" A Deep One, quietly browsing through the 'Fisheries & Wildlife' section, looked up, an expression of mild interest on its piscine features. "—abridged," finished Al, and the Deep One went back to browsing. "*The Pnakotic Manuscripts, Cultes des Goules*…nice copy of *The R'lyeh Text*—"

The customer smiled hopefully.

"—but I've got half-a-dozen copies already. Ditto *De Vermis Mysteriis* and *Dhol Chants*. What's this? *The Necronomicon*."

"Surely *that's* got to be worth something?"

Without turning, Al gestured to the laden shelf behind him. "I've got copies coming out of my eldritch horror, and half of those are first edition, bound in human skin. Yours is just an Arkham House paperback."

The customer didn't bother to hide his disappointment. "So…what *can* you give me for them? I'm really just trying to clear out my attic."

Al shook his head slowly. "Well, I'm afraid I can't really offer—" *anything*, he had been about to say, but something at the bottom of the casket caught his eye. His breath caught in his throat. *It couldn't be!* "—ah, that is," he surreptitiously removed the book from the casket, placing it face down behind the stack on the counter, "I can't offer any more than…say, twenty?"

The customer looked doubtful. "Well…"

"As I say, I've already got most of these, and they're not worth much anyway." Al licked his lips. "Thirty?"

The customer shrugged. "Yeah, okay. Thirty, then."

Al nodded, pulled the Flint of Azathoth and a small glass vial from a drawer, and rolled up his sleeve. Bunching his hand into a fist, he made a small, expert cut across his deeply scarred forearm. "Here we go…" He held his wrist over the vial, allowing a thin dribble of blood to collect therein. "And there's thirty CCs." He rummaged in the drawer again and pulled out a patch of gauze, which he applied to the cut, while the customer sealed the vial and tucked it away in a shirt pocket.

"Well, I guess every little bit counts at the weekly offering," said the customer. *"Cthulhu fhtagn!"* he added, hastily.

"Cthulhu fhtagn!" echoed Al.

The customer nodded, then left, taking the empty casket with him.

Al watched him go. Then, with trembling hands, he picked up his prize, turned it over, and regarded it with feverish eyes. There was no way this was going out on the shelves! It would be locked away, protected by elder signs, to be brought out whenever the moon was gibbous; its every word pored over in minute detail, until the arcane knowledge therein was his.

And then—

Al glanced around at the worm-ridden, ancient shelving; the rotting wood mucous-stained and acid-etched by years of customer abuse. He grinned. There were going to be some changes around here. Oh, yes. *Changes.*

He scanned the title of the book once more.

Better Homes & Gardens—Building Bookcases (A DIY Guide).

Scotoma Fatalis

Denise was nearly halfway to the station before she realised she'd forgotten to ask for the drops to reverse the dilation.

She stopped walking, paused a moment to shift weight from her sore foot, and turned to glare back in the direction of the ophthalmologist's office. Even with her glasses on, everything looked overexposed and somehow *smeared*, as though Doctor Chadwick had rubbed Vaseline into her eyes. She huffed in frustration. She always— *always*—made a point of asking to have the whatchamacallit drops put in to reverse the effects of the dilating drops, after finding herself unable to do anything useful for at least an hour after her first check-up, over a decade ago. It was the damned pain from her foot, she decided. Or the fact she'd had to take public transport for the first time. Or being here without Thomas. The lack of her usual routine; *that* was why she'd forgotten to ask this time around (although why the drops weren't offered automatically was beyond her). She shifted her weight again, and the rubbery surface of the bland modern pathway that followed the train tracks gave slightly under her flats.

Should she go back? She swayed slightly, undecided. It was ten minutes back, maybe just under ten to the station. Her foot was already throbbing again; old age and lack of exercise. Her GP had advised—before telling her to 'tough it out'—that walking daily would eventually get her used to being on her feet. But surely adding an extra thirty minutes to today's trek couldn't be healthy when she was already trying to push through the pain?

Her eyes teared up, and she blinked angrily. What was the book Thomas had once tried to talk to her about, with the long-distance walk where the competitors were executed if they stopped to rest? This must be how *their* feet felt.

Dammit.

There was no point. She would simply have to get home and twiddle her damned thumbs for the next hour or so until the dilation diminished sufficiently for her to be able to do anything worthwhile.

She turned sharply on her heel, wincing, and headed on towards the station.

Thomas would have been able to drive her home. With a bit of light prodding, he would even have turned the car around and taken her back to Doctor Chadwick's to get the reversal drops. By now, she could have been back home already, she and Thomas each immersed in a book; he in one of his frivolous sci-fi publications, her in some gritty Scandi-noir—

Abruptly she remembered the latest Jo Nesbo novel in her bag, which she'd begun on the train in and had been looking forward to sinking back into on the trip back. Instead, she was going to have to spend forty minutes staring blankly out the window at a world which would look as though it had been filmed in soft focus.

Double-damn.

She quickened her pace, despite the growing pain in her foot, and did her best to clamp down on the anger that rose within her. Thomas hadn't even been gone a year, and the stabbing pain of grief and loss had already transmuted into a constant dull sense of frustration over how his absence inconvenienced her on a daily basis; nobody to drive her, or to push the shopping trolley, or to remember to put the bins out. And even the things she *could* do had been lessened. *Reduced.* She now cooked for one. Washed less than half as many clothes, many of those now worn a couple of days in a row. Nobody to share her thoughts with regarding the latest book she was reading.

So this is why people have children, she thought bitterly.

I should have gone first.

She sniffed sharply, then started as the noise was mimicked from somewhere close behind her. A moist sniff. Shuffling footsteps. The sense of someone approaching from behind. She stiffened, gripping her bag more tightly. *The Pensioner Cringe*, she and Thomas had called it; the way silly old folk shrunk back in abject terror from blameless pedestrians. And now, here she was on the verge of doing it herself. *Stupid old woman.*

The shuffling drew level with her shoulder.

Maintaining her pace, Denise moved aside slightly to allow her fellow wayfarer room to pass. In the corner of her eye, a blurred, shaggy-looking mass shuffled and bobbed and edged forward. She took another painful step to the side, teetering on the very edge of the path as she wobbled determinedly towards the station.

'Sorry,' she muttered automatically. *Sorry for taking up space. For getting in your way. For existing.*

A sharp snort of surprise clapped her ears. The shuffling ceased abruptly, the walker vanishing instantly from her peripheral vision as Denise moved on and away. The sudden quiet made her realise how loud the shuffling and snorting had been. Now, just the sounds of distant traffic.

Such a strange reaction, she thought, almost as though she'd surprised him. Had he not noticed her until she spoke? *He*, surely, as the footfalls had seemed too loud and heavy for a woman. She resisted the urge to turn and look behind her; what could she possibly see, anyway? Maybe it had been one of those young people with headphones or whatchamacallit, Bluetooth buds, in their ears. *No*, she thought, furrowing her brow; if that were the case, how had he heard her muttered apology? No sound of resumed walking from behind her, she suddenly realised, and the back of her neck prickled unpleasantly as she pictured the man standing still, staring at her as she strode painfully away.

There was a sudden rush of approaching footsteps from behind, running full-tilt towards her—*at* her—no longer shuffling but striking softly against the path like an Olympic sprinter. The muscles in the back of her neck clenched, ice exploded through her veins, and she stumbled, almost falling. *Not falling*, she thought; *I'm having a fall, because that's what old people do, and I won't be able to get up if I go down!* Her legs wobbled for a moment, the tips of her shoes scraping against the path, then she recovered slightly, breaking into a shaky run to prevent herself from toppling forward. Her arms flailed as she desperately attempted to balance herself, and her outstretched fingers brushed against something that felt like damp, matted fur. She made a strangled noise deep in her throat, and a low *whuff* issued from the dark shape sliding into her periphery.

Denise stumbled on. *If you stop, you'll have to engage with this idiot.* She blinked again, and tried to peer forwards through the medically-induced haze. She couldn't be more than five minutes from the station, and surely this stalker wouldn't do anything so close to all the houses lined up against the opposite side of the street. She risked another sidelong glance. The dark shape bobbed and jerked, moving less like a person and more like one of those Chinese dragons you saw at festivals;, peering here and there, up and down, but never quite *at* Denise.

Drug addict?

Her bowels clenched. An addict wouldn't care if the police were standing right over him; he'd still go through with whatever was running through his addled mind. Maybe she could scream for help? Someone would have to hear her, surely? People would pour out of their houses to help an old lady being mugged—

And then she thought about How The World Was, and realised she was probably on her own.

Yell at him. Ask him what the bloody hell he thinks he's doing. Shame him. Startle him, like you did before. Scare him. He won't expect fire and brimstone from an old lady.

She balled her hands into fists. The wetness coating her fingertips from where she'd touched the man's coat slicked her palms, viscous and warm and unpleasant, like olive oil. She glanced down, staring at the red streaks on her skin. *Paint?* To her bleary vision it looked the colour of—

She shuddered.

Blood? Of a previous victim?

Impossible. There would have been screaming and sirens already. The street wasn't *that* deserted, surely? *You've been reading too much Nesbo.* She risked a quick glance to the side, turning her head to properly regard her tormentor—and almost screamed.

He was looking away from her, head tilted back slightly as though sniffing the air. There was a vague impression of matted fur, a face the texture of bone, stained teeth set in a snout. *A horror mask*, she thought. She choked slightly, and snapped her head back to face forwards as she continued to stumble along the path. In her peripheral vision she saw the awful face turn towards her, dark, hazy holes where eyes should be. It tilted its head to the side, a sharp, jerky movement like a bird might make. Then it jerked again, into a slightly different position. And again. It was as though it wasn't looking directly at her, but was *listening* to her. Or *for* her.

Was it *blind*?

And when, she suddenly wondered, had she began thinking of her unwelcome companion as *it* instead of *him*?

No, that was all so stupid. Blind? It had run swiftly up behind her without stumbling or tripping. And this wasn't one of Thomas' stupid books about monsters and the like. This horrid person was all too human, and all the more frightening for it.

She directed her gaze forward.

Just keep walking. That fuzzy blob ahead of you is the station. She sucked against her dental plate, saliva filling her dry mouth, a slight sound escaping her lips.

Its head jerked again. She automatically glanced sidelong at it, and the pits of its eyes seemed to finally fix upon her. It made a guttural sound, and Denise flinched as wetness spattered her cheek. With it came the stench of—well, she couldn't say exactly what, but it put her in mind of rotten meat and dank cellars and sodden heaps of old grass cuttings. Before she could stop herself, she slapped at the clammy mucous coating the side of her face.

It leaned closer to her with a gurgling hiss.

It can hear me.

It can see, but it can't see me. *But it heard me when I spoke to it. When I sucked my teeth. When I slapped myself. That's how it's locating me. That's how it hunts.*

A sudden recollection of something Thomas had once said, in yet another tedious attempt to engage her interest in something he was a reading; a story about blind prehistoric predators that flew up from the darkness of a newly discovered cave and located their human prey by sound alone.

If I stop making noise—

Denise jolted to a halt, squinting desperately towards the station —so near, yet so horribly far away—only then becoming aware of the now-excruciating throb in her foot. She opened her mouth to gasp, caught herself, bit down on it, gritting her teeth against the agony.

The creature maintained its shambling stride for a few moments, then stopped abruptly a few metres ahead, head darting about. Searching.

Got you, Denise thought, more in relief than triumph. She was too exhausted to gloat. The pain was awful, and she carefully placed a trembling hand over her mouth to stifle her panting. She stood still, swaying slightly, and thought about maybe squatting down to sit on the path. Until someone came along to help. Until the creature went away. She glared, trying to blink her vision clear and get a proper look at it. It shuffled around on the spot in evident confusion, back still turned towards Denise, head twitching back and forth, tilting this way and that. Listening.

This was all quite impossible, Denise thought. Against all that was rational, this *was* exactly like something from one of Thomas' books. This creature roaming the suburbs, especially in full daylight—well, it would have been all over the news. On every TV station, in every newspaper. All over the social media that kept people glued to their phones instead of looking where they were bloody-well going. People would be out hunting it, attempting to catch or kill it. So—

She blinked again. And a thought occurred.

Is this thing…invisible to most people?

Ridiculous.

But…wouldn't that explain why nobody has reported sightings, or screams? Is that why no ill-fated walker has put in a call to the police? Has it been here all along, preying upon pedestrians? One here, one there, over a long period of time? Is that why it's not been in the news?

And—

And am I only seeing it because of my dilated pupils? Because of those accursed eye drops? I've never forgotten to get the effect reversed before. I've never had to walk this path before.

Oh God!

The creature began to turn in a tight circle on the spot. Snuffling. Jerking. Twitching. As it turned further towards Denise she could better make out that monstrous face, even through the blur, like the yellowed skull of a great cat; empty sockets and far too many teeth, maned by the same fur that swept down across its apelike body, seemingly (as far as Denise could make out) stopping just short of the knuckles of long, clawed fingers and thick-toed—*cloven?*—feet.

In spite of her terror, Denise grinned, baring her teeth savagely. *Fooled you. You can't hear me. I can stay as quiet as a mouse, for as long as it takes.*

I beat you!

The creature turned full towards Denise—and froze.

Tightness gripped her chest. *Don't make a sound!*

The creature let out a low growl, soft and menacing.

Stay still! Stay silent!

No—run!

Stupid old lady! You wouldn't get two steps! Her foot felt like a lump of brutalised meat, swollen and raw and pulling her body down.

Denise's hands flew to her mouth, desperately stifling her panicked gasping.

The creature sank into a half-crouch. Then it slowly and carefully took a step forward. Then another. Like a lion stalking a gazelle. The black pits seemed to stare directly into her eyes, and Denise suddenly had no doubt that it could absolutely see her now.

But—

Unbidden—*is this my life flashing before my eyes?*—she suddenly recalled Thomas mentioning yet another book, wherein the author described an alien beast so stupid that it thought if *you* couldn't see *it*, *it* couldn't see *you*.

It hadn't seemed funny then. It didn't seem funny now.

Bloody bastard eye drops!

It sprang.

Denise opened her mouth to shriek, because there was no point doing anything more, or less.

Chrysalis

Consciousness hit him like a hammer. He convulsed, thrashing against silk-lined pine, striking out until the lid above him cracked. Soft, cool soil gushed into his eyes and mouth, and with it came an overwhelming sense of *belonging*, of oneness; the soil, the rocks and himself, all crawling with life, yet lifeless, unfettered by the wretched need to scratch, rub, defecate or breathe. No tics, aches or weariness; just the comforting throb of the earth, the whispering cycles of the soil. Joy overwhelmed him. He tried to cry out, but his desiccated lungs produced only a low moan.

He lay still for a while. Then, driven by an urge to immerse himself completely in the dirt, he clawed at the coffin lid until it came apart under his fingernails, and swam upwards, open-mouthed, allowing the deep, rich loam to penetrate and fill him. Unexpectedly erupting from the earth, he lay trembling upon the ground. *So hot. So bright.* He clawed at the sunbaked ground with hard, dry fingers, moaning, desperately attempting to return to the cooling comfort of the dirt. But the hard topsoil upon which he lay refused to part as the moist sod beneath had done.

Eventually, he clambered to his feet and stood staring miserably at the world around him. Living things scuttled among the headstones and grasses, slithering between leaves and branches, whirring overhead and underfoot. The very air pulsed with life. He moaned again. *Why am I here?*

Voices drifted between the tombs. The world pressed in upon him, and something inside suddenly snapped. He began to run, long, staggering strides propelling him jerkily across the graveyard. He stumbled over a weed-covered drain and fell, bursting out between plots and diving onto a gravel-lined path. He lay still for a moment, savouring the sensation of cold stone against his ruined face.

Someone screamed.

He raised his head. Further up the path stood a woman, her face pale, a crumpled bouquet of flowers clutched between trembling hands. She stared at him, delicate veins pulsing in her throat, muscles twitching beneath her skin.

Self-pity dissolved away.

You poor, wretched creature. Your every moment must be agony. The endless anticipation of bodily failure, of aneurysm, blindness, senility, entombing you forever in a cell of living flesh. If I could do something, anything, to relieve your suffering—

And abruptly, he understood.

He staggered to his feet, and she turned and fled. He pursued her, a new sense of purpose lending him speed.

Wait! Come back! Let me help you!

She darted off the path, stumbling between ancient crypts. He quickened his pace. Then her foot twisted beneath her, and she fell.

He was upon her in a moment, shuddering in revulsion as he caressed her warm flesh, covering her mouth, stifling her cries.

This is my purpose: to take you to a better place. That which I devour will be purified. The rest will rise again to join me in my task...

He bit into her neck, tore, chewed and bit again, moaning rapturously between mouthfuls. And she moaned too, briefly, then fell silent. And after a while, she began to moan again…

Eight-Beat Bar

The turntable was a surprise; a Technics 2005, parked on a shiny chrome stand in the corner. Not the latest model, but a pretty schmick piece of equipment nonetheless. Certainly not the sort of luxury item Jake had expected to find in his three-metre-wide concrete cell. He smiled, recalling the sensation of vinyl spinning under his fingertips. Then he remembered where he was, and stopped smiling. "What's the turntable for?"

"Playin' music on, kid!" Helvis grinned, teeth glittering as brightly as the sequins on his white jumpsuit, and gently pushed Jake towards the chair in the centre of the room; a high-backed monstrosity of aged oak and brass-buckled leather straps, sitting directly under the naked hanging lightbulb. Jake reluctantly took a seat, and Helvis began to strap him in. "See, music's a powerful cosmic force. Tribal. Makes the people come together, y'know? Messes with emotion. Lets you travel in time. You hear 'Video Killed The Radio Star' on the radio, and *bam!* " he snapped his fingers. "You're *there*. Nineteen eighty-three, sittin' in front of the teevee, watchin' MTV, hearin' that song for the first time. A *powerful* force, music."

Jake nodded, smiling condescendingly. "Yeah, I know. I'm a club DJ. *Was* a club DJ."

A pause.

"Yeah, DJ K. I was pretty big. You've probably heard of me."

Helvis raised an eyebrow.

Or not, thought Jake, sourly. "Anyway, yeah, I know what you mean. Music's a powerful force."

"Sure." Helvis' grin widened, not at all reassuringly. "And not just for good…"

Jake glanced at the turntable again, and some unpleasant possibilities began to occur to him.

Helvis nodded. "That's right, kid. Gotta remember, music can rally man 'gainst his fellow man. Break your heart. And heck, *everyone* got a song that just plain drives 'em nuts. How's them straps? Comfortable?"

Jake strained experimentally. "No."

"Cool." Helvis stood up, dusting his hands off theatrically. "Now, 'fore we get started, I gotta explain the rules to you. A legal requirement, kinda."

Jake snorted unbelievingly. "Legalities? Here?"

"Sure, gotta have laws, even here. Otherwise ev'rything goes to Heck, ends up in Chaos, which is a whole diff'rent zipcode. Okay now, listen up. You are here for *eternity*, kid, and condemned to eternal punishment. Ain't no early release for good behaviour. Only chance you got to improve your lot—and I'm talkin' chance-in-a-billion, here——is maybe the punishment ain't effective. That bein' the case, you join the staff, like me. Not a bad gig. Get to meet a whole bunch of people." He winked. "Like I say, chance in a billion. Guys downstairs like me to mention it, though, just to rub it in."

"That's really fucked," Jake muttered.

"Kinda the idea, kid." Helvis shrugged apologetically. "Nothin' personal. Just doin' my job."

Jake sighed. "So, what's the punishment?"

"Well now, see, that's where the music comes in."

"Yeah, well, I'd kind of figured that out already."

"All folks here get the same deal." Helvis jerked his thumb at the turntable. "One song, 'specially picked just for you, playing non-stop for the rest of eternity. Like I said, ev'ryone got at least one song drives 'em nuts, which is what the Selectors are aimin' for. Got a guy next door hates disco, listenin' to a looped recordin' of 'Shake Your Groove Thang'. He screams a lot. Amadeus Mozart? He's here, listenin' to a yodellin' track. Went crazy after the first ten minutes. Selectors know their stuff." He grinned. "Now, if the song don't work, we can mess 'round with it a little. Speed it up, slow it down, play it backwards, anything to push your buttons. What we *can't* do is change the track if *your* song don't work."

Jake nodded thoughtfully. "Okay… So, what's my song?"

"Well, lessee here…" Helvis reached up, made a plucking gesture, and a twelve-inch vinyl record appeared in his hand. "And the magic song is—" he peered at the record label, "—'Altered States', by GK. Ampland Mix, 2006. Huh. Seems I recall this tune was pretty popular. Thirty-two weeks on the charts, or somesuch. You really hate it, huh?" He glanced up, and noted Jake's expression. "What?"

Jake hesitated, a smug smile frozen on his face.

"C'mon, what?" Helvis urged.

"Just to clarify," said Jake, cautiously, "now that the song's been picked, you can't change it, right?"

Helvis nodded. "Sure. So why you lookin' so pleased with y'self?"

"Well, it's just that I don't actually hate that song. At least, no more so than hundreds of other songs."

Helvis' eyes glittered. "So why'd the Selectors pick it out, y'think?"

Jake shrugged. "Dunno. It's actually a pretty good song. Catchy. I liked it a lot when it first came out." He paused. "But…well, you know how it is when a song gets really popular. Gets played on the radio ten times a day, which kind of kills the enjoyment. And clubbers. Do you know what a pain in the arse clubbers can be? I mean, when a song gets popular you play it at least once a night, of course. But five minutes after you play it, some idiot always comes up and asks you to play it again. But you can't keep playing the same song over and over, because anyone who *doesn't* like that song is going to piss off, and management doesn't like to see drink sales walking out. So people come up to the DJ booth, asking over and over to hear songs like 'Oh What A Night', or 'Horny', or 'Altered States', and you tell them you can't—politely, I mean, just explaining how it is—but they don't fucking *listen*, just keep coming back every five minutes, asking over and over for you to play the bloody song, and eventually you've just got to tell them to fuck off, and then they get nasty, so you end up hating not only clubbers but also the song they were asking for by association, and the fact it keeps playing on the radio 'cos it's on the charts for *thirty two fucking weeks—!*" He broke off, red-faced.

A pause.

"So, you *really* hate that song, huh?"

Jake nodded gloomily. "Guess so…"

Helvis nodded sympathetically. "Well, anyway, it's great you can rationalise *why* you hate it so much. Maybe it'll help some."

Jake smiled weakly. "Thanks."

"Hey, no problem, kid. Like I said, got nothin' 'gainst you personally, just doin' my job is all. Don't mean I can't be civil." Helvis walked over to the turntable, switched it on, set the record down, and carefully positioned the needle. There was a pause. Then the familiar intro kicked in; eighties-style electronica quickly leading into a modern bass-thumping dance beat.

"Heartbeat recalls
"Ancient ichthyic rhythms.
"In sleep the mind
"Roams ancestry—"

Helvis turned the volume up slightly, then regarded Jake again. "Be back to check on you in a while," he said. "But I don't think you'll be in any state to appreciate it by then." Smiling, he turned and left the room.

Jake strained against his straps for a moment, then slumped resignedly back in his chair.

"—Primeval ocean
"The blood remembers.
"Breathe the waters.

"Return with me."

It was jarring at first. The same lyrics, over and over. Grating on his nerves. eventually getting so bad that he began to snuffle like a self-pitying child, moaning and mumbling, eyes watering. Unsurprisingly, this did nothing to lessen the pain. Changing tactics, Jake tried blocking the lyrics from his mind. And it worked. For a time, there was only the beat. Eight beats to the bar. Four bars to the verse. A familiar rhythm. Soothing. Comforting.

But eventually, the repetitive thud of the bass began to weigh upon his mind, drowning his thoughts. Boredom set in. Deep, *painful* boredom.

Jake began to snuffle again.

God! Anything *to relieve the boredom! I would* kill—*literally* kill—*for a copy of 'Let's Go Crazy' to mix into this. That mix always went down well…*

He smiled, remembering. And then a thought occurred…

Some time later—Days? Years? Centuries?—Helvis stuck his head around the corner. "Lookin' good, kid! What gives?"

Jake shrugged coyly.

Helvis seemed a little put out. "Well. Okay, then. Let's try speedin' it up—"

"Go for your life. Won't make a difference."

Helvis raised an eyebrow. "Yeah? Why's that, kid?"

Jake hesitated.

Helvis spread his hands wide. "Hey! Can't change the song, so where's the harm in tellin' me where the Selectors went wrong?" He smiled encouragingly.

Jake eyed Helvis thoughtfully, then nodded. "Okay, here it is—I'm a really good DJ."

"And…?"

Jake shook his head. "No. I mean, I'm a *really* good DJ. Got the magic touch. I can get the toughest crowd up and dancing, or clear the floor at the end of the night, or make people head up to the bar to buy drinks. You know why?"

Helvis shrugged.

"Because I'm open-minded. Most DJs only play the sort of stuff *they* like to hear, which is usually a pretty narrow selection. Me, I play *anything*. Rock, pop, disco, dance, golden oldies. Anything that'll get them up and dancing."

"Must play a heckuva lot of stuff you don't enjoy."

"Sure. But it doesn't *matter* to me if I don't like a particular song —it's the end result of *playing* that song that gives me the buzz. A sense of *power*. Knowing that I can control every last person in the club."

Helvis glanced pointedly around the room. "No crowd here, kid."

Jake shrugged again. "Doesn't matter. I can *imagine* the crowd. *Remember* the buzz."

"Real commendable. Still, the song you like least of all, played over and over for eternity—" Helvis shrugged. "Might not shred your nerves, but boredom can drive you mad too, kid."

Jake smiled smugly. "Well. The *other* reason I'm such a shit-hot DJ is that I've got *imagination*. I am the *king* of music formatting. I can *feel* what songs complement each other, which tracks mix best into other specific tracks, so I'm always coming up with new combinations. My playlist *evolves*, which keeps it fresh and exciting."

"One song ain't a playlist, kid. Won't be doin' no mixin' in here."

"Not *physically*, no." Jake smiled. "But while that song's playing, I'm mentally running through every other song I know—that's literally thousands of songs, hundreds of thousands of combinations of songs —and imagining myself mixing, cutting, fading, looping and scratching them in over the top of 'Altered States'. I reckon I've got enough in my head to entertain me for eternity. You can play that bloody song faster, slower, backwards, whatever you like, but as long as it's got an eight-beat bar—"

Something in Helvis' eyes changed.

"What?" asked Jake, suspiciously.

Helvis held up the ring-encrusted index finger of his right hand. "So. Get a kick out of *scratching*, huh, kid?"

"Heartbeat recalls

"Ancient ichthyic rhythms—"

Helvis stepped towards the turntable, reached out, and almost casually drew his fingernail across the spinning record.

"—t ich—

"—t ich—

"—t ich—"

No tune. No structure. Just a beat-and-a-half of discordant gibberish. Like fingernails across a blackboard.

"Annoyin', ain't it?" Helvis gave a small, self-satisfied smirk. "I bet even a hot-shot DJ like you can't do nothin' with *that*." He sauntered past Jake, and stood framed in the doorway for a moment, looking back. "Enjoy, kid."

Soon afterwards, Jake began to scream.

Tagged

Clancy was uncharacteristically quiet as he sat across the carriage from Trev; greasy grey beard spilling down over his bulging, sweat-stained shirt, navy tie loosened now they were no longer before the magistrate, face drawn and pale. Not at all like the cheerful, chatty character Trev knew from the Longbeach Hotel get-togethers. Odd, given he'd only just walked from court with all charges dropped. Unless—

The altercation with the old woman couldn't *still* be upsetting him, could it?

What a fuckin' sook. The epithet made Trev think about some of the things he'd heard in court that day. He didn't really know Clancy that well. Just an acquaintance of the same general vintage, moving in the same circles, with whom Trev shared an occasional beer in the company of a dwindling group of similarly-aged hard boys. And while the boys had always delighted in pointing out that Trev and Clancy might have passed for brothers thirty years earlier, Clancy was now just a couple of decent meals away from obesity, while Trev had managed to maintain most of his bulk as muscle, which was why Clancy had asked Trev to play escort that day.

"Not expecting trouble," Clancy had said over the phone. *"But you know how people get aggro over this sort of thing. Better to have muscle along, for after it all gets thrown out."*

He'd sounded confident, and Trev said so.

"Charges are crap, that's why."

And they're not going to put a kid on the stand, Trev had thought, matter-of-factly. He'd assumed Clancy was innocent; less due to friendly loyalty, more due to the fact that most of the old mob were family men now, and would probably have made Clancy disappear if there'd been any serious suspicions of guilt.

"There's a hundred bucks and a six-pack for you to get me to court, then back home to Frankston. Having you there should put anyone off being a have-a-go hero. Just one old hag I'm maybe expecting trouble from, so it's easy money."

In Trev's experience, there was no such a thing as 'easy money'. But, because jobs were becoming few and far between for an aging enforcer with arthritis and diabetic retinopathy, he'd agreed.

Now Trev slumped back in his seat, swaying with the motion of the train as he looked at Clancy and thought about some of the things that had been said in court. Then he tried to not think about them, turning away to gaze at nothing, allowing The Bleed to fill his vision; a blob of crimson that darted back and forth with every twitch of his right eye. *Leave it too much longer,* his ophthalmologist had warned, *and you'll risk full blindness.* But the idea of undergoing the surgery…

Trev shivered, blinking the red haze away, his gaze drifting to the graffiti behind Clancy, following the fluid, grainy lines and loops and whorls. Fucking disrespectful. *"This Is Mine!"* Yet always on someone else's property. More than one of Trev's early jobs had been to sort out the local kids who'd picked the wrong wall to tag. Here on the train, the spattered spray-painting really stuck out like the proverbial, jarringly at odds with the too-clean floors, cream walls, and nasty-modern blue-print seats.

"Now arriving at…Edithvale," chimed the recorded female voice, as the train squealed to a halt. Morose-looking commuters tugged at the doors, spilling out into the winter chill beyond, leaving Trev and

Clancy's end of the carriage largely unoccupied. The doors grated shut. The train lurched forward, the rusty grinding of wheels quickly fading to a low hum.

Trev glanced at Clancy again, wondering. He was old enough and ugly enough to know that you couldn't always pick a rock-spider. They looked just like everyone else. Sometimes, though, there was a vibe. He didn't get that vibe from Clancy, but—

He thought again about some of the testimonies. The stories from near-hysterical parents. The way they'd described Clancy. The mannerisms. The way he spoke. That sounded *exactly* like the Clancy Trev knew. And then the descriptions of what they said he'd done…

The faint tang of bile rose in Trev's gullet, and he sucked up a mouthful of saliva to wash the taste away.

Clancy sat up suddenly, and began to pat himself down, sweaty hands exploring nooks and pockets. "Hey!"

Trev blinked irritably. "What?"

"Did she have anything? The old lady?"

Trev stared at Clancy.

"Like, in her hands? Did she put anything on me?"

Trev furrowed his brow, feeling a twinge of shame. He was a pro, and proud of it. But the old bitch had made him look incompetent, dodging around him, a flail of faded fabric and wrinkled flesh. He simply hadn't seen her. She'd seemed to blend in with the stonework of the courthouse wall, like a spider against bark. Was his eyesight really that bad now?

Had she had something in her hand?

Trev felt a sharp pain in his own hands, and looked down to find he'd balled them into tight, arthritic fists. He hissed slightly, unclenched them.

"Like, what? A weapon?"

Trev suddenly felt very tired. He didn't want to be here. Didn't want to be talking to Clancy, or thinking about today or the old hag or the things that had been said in court. Nor of the row of parents, sat along the back of the courtroom, their eyes boring into the back of Trev and Clancy's heads. He wanted to be at home, on the couch, drinking beer, watching TV under the dim loungeroom light that took the edge off The Bleed.

"No!" Clancy snapped. "Like—*anything*. Anything at all. A necklace? Beads?"

Trev stared at Clancy with more contempt than he would have thought possible. "Beads? Fucking *beads??*" His hands automatically curled back into fists. He ignored the pain. "What's she gonna do with fucking *beads??*"

"Or whatever!" Clancy snapped back, glaring at the floor. He made a dismissive gesture, gave his pockets a final pat down, then slumped, looking sick and miserable. Trev hoped Clancy wasn't about to keel over and die. He needed that hundred.

"Now arriving at…Chelsea."

Trev forced his gaze away from Clancy, quietly exhaling his rage, and felt his fists relax slightly. He tried focussing upon the graffiti on the opposite wall of the carriage, but his mind's eye threw up a replay of the old lady *darting around you with ease, slapping at Clancy's face and neck with splayed, spiderlike hands, hissing viciously. Clancy makes a noise like a stuck pig, and Trev jumps in between them, giving the old bitch a shove that parks her on her arse several metres away. But she doesn't scream. She just stares at Clancy, and smiles a slow, nasty smile that stretches from ear to ear. Trev grabs Clancy's sweaty, quivering arm and hauls him off towards La Trobe station before the people yelling nearby can find sufficient moral outrage to have a go.*

Trev snorted, staring out the window, letting his silence answer Clancy's query.

"She's into some weird shit," said Clancy, eventually.

Trev waited for elaboration, but Clancy just turned away and stared out the window.

Are you *into some weird shit, Clancy?*

It was past 6pm now, and growing dark. The houses and trees beyond the window had become little more than smears of off-white against dark grey, rushing past in a blur.

"Now arriving at…Bonbeach."

Buffeted in his seat as the train took off again, Trev had the fleeting impression that the tags on the wall opposite were undulating. He blinked, and the graffiti settled into stillness. Pretty-much all the tags down this end of the carriage had been done by the same 'artist'; dozens of football-sized oval lozenges, the colour of dried blood, each filled with weird foreign lettering. Different lettering in each, Trev realised. Weren't tags supposed to be the signature of the artist? So shouldn't they all be identical?

He stared through The Bleed, and the tags seemed to shift again, falling into patterns that put Trev in mind of honeycomb, or the scales of a gigantic reptile.

A mild sense of vertigo washed over him. He shook his head slightly, then scanned the length of the carriage. The artist had been busy in here. Almost every inch of the carriage wall had been tagged.

Had there been so many when he and Clancy came aboard?

Trev craned around to look behind him. There, too. *Fucking kids. Kids…*

"What're you looking at?"

Trev started. "Nothing," he snapped. And then, more to vent than to promote conversation: "Fuck's up with you, anyway?"

Clancy glared back for a moment, then sagged. "That woman," he began, then stopped, rubbing a thumb against his lips and looking back out of the window. It was almost pitch-black outside now.

Don't talk, thought Trev. *Don't talk, don't talk, don't talk.* "Ah, stop your fucking whingeing!" he snapped. "She was just some old bitch!"

"Yeah, and a fucking great job *you* did keeping her off me!" Clancy shot back.

"Now arriving at…Carrum," chimed the loudspeaker.

Trev's knuckles tightened, then cracked, sharp pain startling him out of what might have been a killing moment. He refocussed his anger on the fact that Clancy clearly wasn't being straight with him about something. An enforcer didn't have to know everything in order to be effective, but did need to know enough to avoid surprises.

"So, what?" he asked, through gritted teeth. "She connected, or something?"

Clancy waved a hand at Trev in a manner that might have indicated a lack of knowledge, or a suggestion to shut up, or both.

Trev leaned forward, pushing his face into Clancy's. *"What?"* he snarled.

Clancy jerked his head back, staring, frightened, like he finally realised how close he was to getting belted.

Good, thought Trev.

"Now arriving at…Seaford." The doors opened, closed again, cutting off the tinny ticking of the last few Ipods and smart phones.

"Listen," Clancy said, desperately. "Look. Let me tell you. I did a stint of community service at her place a while back. Painting fences, fixing hinges. That sort of shit. House looked like something out of a horror movie. Run down. Creepy as fuck. Full of stray cats she was feeding. Other weird shit. Not the sort of person or place you'd want your kids hanging around, right? Not these days…"

Nah, thought Trev. *Not these days. Maybe once, when we were kids. When you could run off and spend the day at a neighbour's without even telling your parents, come home after dark, and nobody worried. When your parents might tell you to go around to the local Crazy Cat-Lady's place, offer to do chores. But not these days.*

Not with people like you *around, Clancy…*

"Yeah," he grunted. "Not these days."

Clancy nodded. "Yeah. But, thing is, local kids loved going around there. Parents, too. Whole neighbourhood loved her. Offering to do chores. Bringing over supplies and meals. And anyone I asked just said she'd been great for the community, that she'd fixed some issues they'd had back when the area was a bit rough. Local hero. So I figured she'd be useful to keep on side. Probably people told her things that might be useful to…our sort of people. Y'know? I kept going over to help out after the community service was done. Maintenance, sometimes just chatting. Helping the kids with their chores, or taking them on errands if they needed adult supervision. But then someone started slinging mud. Things got nasty."

Trev grunted, looking at the tags.

"Old bitch finally came and asked. She'd got it into her head that I'd done the things they said. Lying fuckers. And I told her no way, not me, 'cos—y'know. Hadn't done anything. But she said I was lying. She said I'd have my day in court. And she said that'd be my last chance to come clean. And if I didn't…"

There was a long pause.

"What?" Trev prompted.

"She said she'd put a curse on me."

Trev stared at Clancy.

"She's…a witch."

Trev stared a moment longer, then snorted derisively, turning away to eye the last couple of commuters at the far end of the carriage.

"No, really! I've seen her…do things! Kid fell down and split his knee open. She took him into her kitchen, this dark, dirty room, and bent down and put her hand on the wound—gushing, it was—and she mumbled some stuff and took her hand away *and it was all healed up!*"

Trev shook his head, not bothering to look at Clancy.

"I watched through the window!" Clancy persisted. "Crack in the window, so she wouldn't see me. But…I reckon maybe she knew I was there. And this one time, I looked through the keyhole, and she brought a dead cat back to life—"

"Clancy?"

"What?"

"Just…shut the fuck up."

Clancy was silent for a moment.

"Now stopping at…Kananook."

"And I heard from one of the parents that once there'd been this guy who was hassling local business owners, and the old lady hexed him, and he disappeared!"

"So," Trev said, slowly, "the old lady threatened to put a curse on you? Stick pins in a voodoo doll? Send the bogeyman 'round?"

"It's not funny!"

"So, if you really believe all this shit, why didn't you do what the old lady said, and come clean in court?"

"BECAUSE I DIDN'T DO IT!"

Bullshit, Trev thought, vaguely realising he'd finally made his mind up about Clancy on several levels. *You didn't come clean because—away from that house and whatever the hell you think you saw through the window, and this being a nice sunny day—you suddenly felt it was all a bit silly, and that maybe you'd imagined it, and that the very real threat of going to jail outweighed the notion that a creepy old lady could use black magic against you. But now, with her coming at you outside of court, and the darkness outside the train, and with time to think about all the stuff you think you saw...*

Trev shook his head in disgust, and glanced again towards the remaining travellers at the far end of the carriage; two small figures in grey hoodies, slumped together in the seats reserved for elderly passengers, cowled faces downturned.

Clancy followed Trev's gaze. "Who's that? Who *is* that?"

"Kids," said Trev, meaning *teens,* of course, but realising as he said it that the figures were far too small to be teenagers. "Just kids," he reiterated, thickly.

Unaccompanied, on a train?

Clancy rose sloppily to his feet, swaying with the motion of the carriage. "Go and see!" he urged.

"Fuck off." Trev's head felt like lead. The Bleed filled his eyes. He just wanted to get off the train.

"Please!" Clancy sobbed. "Go and look! I'll give you another hundred!" He fumbled at his back pocket, dropping his wallet and spilling its contents across the floor. With a groan, he sank painfully to his knees to retrieve his belongings, not taking his eyes off the hooded figures. "Please! Just go and check!"

"THEY WERE JUST FUCKING KIDS!!" Trev roared.

Clancy whimpered, scraping credit cards and notes and coins towards him.

And then Trev saw it.

On the back of Clancy's sweat-stained collar: a thumb-sized replica of the tags crowding the carriage wall. Blurred, like The Bleed.

No, Trev realised: *smeared.* Applied in haste to a moving target.

"The next station will be...Frankston. This train will...terminate...at Frankston."

Trev rose automatically, moving quickly to the nearest exit. Swaying, he placed a steadying hand against the door, turned slightly, and saw the little hooded figures standing with their backs towards him at the very end of the carriage. A fumbling of baggy sleeves, a sputtering hiss, and both figures moved away towards their nearest exit.

A wet, red tag glinted against the Perspex of the inter-carriage door.

"Now arriving at...Frankston. Terminating at...Frankston."

The train lurched as it ground to a halt.

Trev squinted. Through The Bleed, the tags shifted stealthily. And kept shifting.

"I'M SORRY!" screamed Clancy. *"I'M SORRY!"*

The doors opened. Trev stepped out, dimly aware of the hooded figures doing the same.

"DON'T LEAVE ME!" screamed Clancy, and then a vicious wind swept along the platform, snatching whatever else he might have said away from Trev's ears. The door hissed closed. The train began to move again, rolling slowly towards the darkened sidings beyond the far end of the station.

Trev stumbled as the wind slapped at him, turning him on his heel to face the train. He threw up a hand to shield his eyes, and saw—

Well, he wasn't sure *what* he saw, really. Clancy was hammering at the window, his screaming drowned out by the squeal of the train's wheels, which horrifyingly seemed to emanate from Clancy's gaping mouth. But for a moment it seemed to Trev—as he squinted through the wind, and The Bleed, and the sudden flickering of the carriage lights as the train pulled away—that the tags inside the carriage had darkened and swelled together like cells under a microscope, stretching out from the walls towards Clancy, moving to engulf him like the mouth of some great anemone—

And then there were just a couple of red lights receding into the night.

The wind died abruptly.

Trev stood staring along the empty tracks for a moment, then scanned the platform up and down, looking for—

But he was completely alone.

Schrödinger's Catastrophe

'Holy shit!'

Jim switched off the projected quantum field surrounding the sealed plastic crate and checked the readings. Then he checked them again. Then, trembling slightly, he cleared his throat and turned to the nearest camera.

"Schrödinger's Stasis Wave, test number…uhm…five-seven-two. The, ah…subject inside the enclosure no longer demonstrates any accepted signs of life. No respiration. No heartbeat or pulse. Even cellular activity is rapidly slowing, according to the readings. And yet—"

Jim glanced towards the observation window. "And yet, we're still registering *movement*. Quite *significant* movement. The subject is basically…pacing up and down inside the enclosure! *Holy shit*." He laughed nervously. "Sorry. Poor choice of words for the official record, but…I think we've *done* it! We've achieved a perfect state of quantum superposition! We have a subject that's paradoxically both alive and dead simultaneously! Holy shit, the applications—"

Jim stopped and took a deep breath. 'Ok, sorry—getting ahead of myself. Let's get the physical exam done.' He moved to the medical cart beside the door and picked up a pair of latex gloves, pulling them on as he entered the testing room. 'This is amazing! Thank you, Erwin Schrödinger, for the inspiration...!'

Inside the crate the undead cat paced restlessly, glaring into darkness with milky eyes. Waiting for the crate to be opened. Waiting to feed.

The Gift

I want to tell you about the third-worst thing that ever happened to me.

It was a Saturday afternoon towards the end of summer last year (as I write this), and still warm enough that I could wash the car on the front driveway in just my shorts and a tee. Sarah was inside (reading, I think), and Max was up in his room, plugged into whatever he was plugging into a year ago. There was a light breeze, which I liked because I was carrying quite a bit more weight back then, and even the relatively low-impact task of rubbing a sponge over the bonnet was getting me a bit overheated.

I'm much thinner now. Lack of appetite.

Anyway.

I was feeling happy that day, probably for the first time since Mum had passed almost a year earlier. It hadn't been unexpected; mesothelioma, from an asbestos-ridden house she'd lived in as a teen during the 1950s. The payout from the company responsible had funded a course of immunotherapy that ended up giving Mum five more years of life than had originally been predicted; five years to say all the things that most people never think to say to their loved ones before it's too late. It had been a gift, I suppose. So, when she finally passed, there were no regrets over things left unsaid. Regardless, it certainly hadn't been a happy time. On this particular day, though, the warmth, and the smell of spring flowers, and the sound of birds and of kids playing further up the street had pushed away the lingering sense of loss, and I was thinking instead about the family holiday to Tasmania we were planning, and how much I was looking forward to taking Max out to the pub for his upcoming eighteenth, and how *comfortable* it felt to be back in the beautiful Victorian-era house I'd grown up in, thanks to a sizeable inheritance.

Maybe that's why it happened; being back where the second-worst thing that ever happened to me had occurred.

I bent over the bucket to re-soak the sponge, huffing slightly, and suddenly felt odd and unsteady. It was as though the world around me suddenly *shifted* slightly, like when you step out of a pub and the night air reacts with the alcohol you just drank inside. I straightened up, dropping the sponge, and pressed my hand against the side of the car for support. The weird sensation persisted, and I briefly wondered whether I was having some sort of medical issue. However, after a few moments the feeling faded, so I mentally shrugged and decided—in the time-honoured tradition of men and their health—to ignore what had just occurred. I turned to give the car a once-over. And that's when I saw the man standing at the end of the driveway, staring at me.

He was tall and slim, and wearing—

Sarah often ribs me for having so much kitsch apparel in my wardrobe, which is fair enough. My parents had both been quite fashionable back in the 60s and 70s, and I'd grown up loving their clothes: the leather, the skivvies, even the corduroy and flares. And after the second-worst thing that ever happened to me, I'd found comfort in keeping the bulk of Dad's wardrobe, much of which I eventually grew into in my late teens and pretended to wear just to get a rise from my mates (which it did) but actually because I genuinely loved the clothes. I'd never had the heart to get rid of most of the attire, despite becoming too fat to fit into it by the time I hit thirty. So now all those amazing retro garments hung in a wardrobe in the spare bedroom, or sat in sealed boxes in the garage.

The man at the end of my driveway looked like he'd dressed up out of those boxes.

His clothes seemed to be in really good condition; far better than old apparel from an op-shop, and I wondered whether he was actually showcasing the latest retro fashion. He wore brown lace-up shoes and dark brown slacks. His shirt was a lighter brown with a faint paisley pattern, and brown buttons up the front. Over this he wore a late 60s-style slim-cut black leather jacket.

My dad had had one just like it when I was a kid.

I looked at the man's face. I guessed he was about a decade younger than me, maybe fortyish, but it was hard to pin an exact age on him due to the thick hipster beard that obscured his jawline. His long hair fell to just shy of his shoulders in thick chestnut locks. His eyes were light blue; I could tell that even from this distance because he had them open very wide, staring at me in what looked like utter bafflement.

The overall vibe of the guy was of someone well-dressed, but for entirely the wrong decade, and possibly a little unhinged, which is why I acknowledged him cautiously.

"Hey, mate," I said, nodding amiably. "You okay there?" There was something familiar about him, and I wondered if he was a neighbour I'd seen before but not interacted with.

He blinked, then turned slightly to stare at the numbered letterbox we'd recently put in to replace the rusting monstrosity that had sat there for the previous forty-five years. "I'm…sorry," he said, not yet looking back at me. His voice also sounded maddeningly familiar; deep, and somehow comforting. I took a couple of steps forward, trying to get a better look at his face. He glanced up and down the street before running his gaze across the front of the house. "I'm—look, this is going to sound stupid, but I think I'm, ah, a bit lost. I thought…I actually thought this was *my* house, but—"

And then he looked at me again.

I locked eyes with him. And suddenly I *knew* him.

My legs began to tremble. I opened my mouth to speak, but found I couldn't draw breath, as the word on my lips swelled to fill my head until it blanked out everything else:

Dad??

On October 2nd, 1979—just five days before my ninth birthday—my dad went out for an early evening walk. And vanished.

I don't remember many actual details about that day, or the months that followed; it all became a sort of blur of awfulness that slowly faded over time. It took a couple of days for the police to take an interest, despite increasingly desperate calls from my mother. No, he wasn't the sort of man to just piss off on a whim *("You'd be surprised how many families think that in these situations, Mrs McKenzie"),* or to go out boozing with mates, or any of the other neat little excuses the police offered up to an increasingly terrified wife and child. "Just a walk along the beach," was the last thing Mum says he told her, as he headed out around five that evening. He did this several times a week; for fitness, he said, though I've since suspected also just to get some alone time. It would have taken him twenty minutes to get there from home, maybe half an hour up and down the foreshore, twenty minutes back. He'd taken nothing with him apart from his wallet and keys. No passport. No extra clothes. His bank accounts remained untouched afterwards. The local paper ran small pieces on the case for a while. But days became weeks, then months, and the story died, and friends and family began to quietly distance themselves from our trauma. The police updated us less and less frequently, and finally not at all. And that was that. No answers. No closure. So we did what had to be done to allow ourselves to move on. We packed away Dad's stuff; all of his clothes and personal belongings, with the exception of his books and records, which remained on the bookshelves in the loungeroom, simply filling the space, and which we never again pulled down to read or listen to. We hid away the framed photos and photo albums, which we each occasionally dug out and cried over when the other wasn't around. We stopped talking about him, though the memory of him remained like a dagger through our hearts. He became a hole in the story of our lives; one that we never again openly acknowledged. Not even through Mum's final years.

And standing there on the driveway, with a lifetime of suppressed anguish punching me in the heart and head, all I could say, eventually, was: "Why don't you come inside…"

"Should we call the police?" asked Sarah, quietly. I nodded, still staring at our guest as I stood by the loungeroom door, from where I'd judged we could keep an eye on him while speaking privately. After a moment, Sarah said: "I can do it, if you like. And I'll ask Max to stay in his room for a bit, so you can…" She trailed off, gazing at the man sitting on our couch, hands on his knees as he stared at his surroundings.

It struck me at that moment just how little the room had changed in almost 45 years. Most of the furniture had been replaced over the decades, but the room still featured the Victorian architraves Dad had stripped and repainted in 1975. There was the now-threadbare green carpet he'd had laid around 1978. At the top of the stained-glass windows facing out onto the road there was still a crack in one panel, where Dad had bumped it with a ladder while replacing a light globe in the pendant light that still hung from the three-metre-high ceiling, back in…the early 70s? And his books and records still lined the shelves.

I became aware of Sarah gently touching my shoulder. "Charlie?"

"Sorry, what?"

"It really can't be *him*. Can it? He'd be over eighty, wouldn't he? This guy's younger than *you*."

I shrugged helplessly. "It *can't* be him. I must be losing my marbles. But—" I swallowed, feeling sick and stupid. "He doesn't just look exactly like Dad—he looks exactly like Dad would have done *on the day he vanished!*"

"Would have done?"

"I didn't *see* him that day! I mean, I *saw* him, but I didn't take note of what he was wearing! Why would I? But those clothes—I remember him wearing those clothes when I was a kid! Not just *similar*—fucking *identical!* And—" I paused, beginning to hyperventilate, "—and he's the *same—fucking—AGE!* Like he walked out of nineteen seventy-nine, and straight into *now!*" I was shaking, and leaned against the doorframe to steady myself as I looked at Sarah, waiting for her to come up with an explanation that *actually made sense*; that this was just a stranger with an uncanny resemblance to my dad, or that I was confused due to stress over Mum's death. Something. Anything. But instead, she just nodded. "Okay. I'll go call the police. I won't tell them that last bit, though, okay? We can deal with all that when they get here. And—" she gestured helplessly. "Are you okay?"

I snorted. "Not even slightly."

She patted my arm. "Tea?"

"Yeah. Please. White with two sugars for him." The words were out of my mouth before I could even consider them.

Sarah hesitated, then kissed me on the cheek and walked away, pulling her phone out of her pocket.

I stared at the man sitting in the loungeroom, balling my hands into fists to try and dispel the shakes. Then I forced what I hoped would look like a comforting smile, and walked into the room.

"So, um…Sarah—that's my wife—is making us a cup of tea. Are you feeling any better? You…seem like you've had a bit of a shock." *You and me both.*

He didn't answer, his gaze darting between myself and various elements of the room. He looked horribly confused, but utterly lucid—not at all like he was drunk, or drugged, or suffering from mental illness—and for some reason that really scared me.

"There's a lot of stuff here that…looks like my stuff," he said eventually, frowning.

"Okay," I said, and then didn't know where to go from there. "You said…you got lost, or something? Do you remember your address?"

"Yes, of course" he said, and named the address we were currently at.

My gut did a slow flip. "Okay. Okay. And do you remember where you were, or what you were doing before you got lost?"

No answer, Instead, he rose from the couch and slowly walked over to the collection of vinyl stacked sideways on the shelf. He reached out and touched the spine of one of the albums. "Bach. Toccata and Fugue in D Minor, performed by Ferdinand Klinda," he murmured. "My copy still has the price sticker on the back…" He carefully pulled the sleeve out halfway. Looked at the back. Slowly pushed the album back into place. "I took a walk, then headed back home," he began, then stopped and looked up at the nearest bookshelf. "Good collection. I've got quite a personal library as well. I'm a high school literature teacher, so…lots of plays and classics. The same editions you have here, by the looks of it." He turned back to face me, his expression stern. "Look. I'm not accusing you of anything," he said slowly. "But if I were to pull down some of these books, would I find…extensive notes inside? Written in biro?"

A beat.

I nodded. I felt like throwing up.

He looked down at the floor. "Notes…that *I* wrote?"

It wasn't really a question.

"Yes." I could hardly speak above a whisper. I didn't want to answer him. Because to do so meant to accept the reality of this whole impossible, terrifying situation.

"These are my things." Another non-question. "And you…" He stared at me again, then looked down at the cluster of framed photos sitting on the coffee table; some recent, some digitally reprinted from the originals that had remained trapped for decades in albums at the back of a dark cupboard. Me with Sarah and Max, all looking rather serious. Me as a late teen with Mum, both smiling gently, our eyes sad.

Me as a child with Mum and Dad; all beaming, enveloping each other in a three-way bear hug, as though determined to never let one another go.

He stared at that last one for what seemed an eternity. Then he looked up at me and asked, quietly:

"Charles?"

I hadn't gone by 'Charles' in over thirty years. Even Mum had called me 'Charlie'.

I nodded, my cheeks suddenly wet. "Yeah. It's me, Dad."

He stared at my face, taking in every detail. Then he swayed slightly, caught himself, and walked back to the couch to sit down. I wanted to rush to him. To hug him. But I couldn't move. I was vaguely aware of voices elsewhere in the house, Sarah speaking in low tones, Max sounding more high-pitched and querulous.

"What *happened?*" Dad asked, eventually. He sat staring blankly ahead of him, looking like a lost child. "How—" he looked up at me again, "—you're so…*old*. Sorry. I'm sorry, I mean…" There was another long pause. Then he seemed to pull himself together somewhat. "So…*when* is this?"

Smart man. Just as I'd remembered.

I slowly walked over to the armchair opposite the couch and sat down. "I don't know what's happened, Dad. You've…been missing since nineteen seventy-nine. October second."

He furrowed his brow. "But…that's *today.*"

"It's February eighteenth, Dad." I tried to blink away my tears. "Twenty twenty-three."

The silence that followed was awful.

He stared at me again, perhaps seeking the boy who should be turning nine in less than a week, and seeing only a bearded, weeping stranger, worn down by the decades he'd missed. "Where's your mum?"

I let out a sob. "She's gone, Dad. Last year."

His face seemed to crumple, skin grey with shock. And suddenly I was absolutely furious, as though a pit filled with forty years of hurt and sorrow and fear and anger had opened up within me. "What the fuck *happened*, Dad? *Where were you??*" I jumped to my feet, fists clenched. "*WHERE DID YOU GO?? YOU LEFT US!!*"

I didn't realise I'd begun shouting until Sarah called out, her voice full of concern. Seconds later, I heard urgent footsteps from upstairs,

Dad shook his head desperately. "I don't *know!* I'm *sorry*, I don't *know!* I don't *know*! I walked along the foreshore, and it started to get dark, and I began walking back, and someone—" He stopped abruptly, placing his hands over his eyes in a gesture of utter misery and despair.

My heart broke, a wave of shame washing over me. What the hell was I doing? Against all logic, I had my dad back! I'd been given a fantastic and impossible gift, and here I was, screaming like a spoiled child! Boundless opportunities for the future flashed through my mind: reconnecting with my dad, folding him back into the family, picking up where he and I had left off, filling him in on the forty-plus years he'd missed. There would be time to discuss what had occurred, to uncover the mystery, to move on, to explore the weirdness of my having a father who was now younger than myself!

Regardless of this bizarre new reality, *we'd have our lives back!*

I rushed over to Dad and squatted down in front of him, grabbing his wrists and pulling his hands away from his face.

His eyes were utterly black, like those of a shark.

And then he *screamed.*

His mouth opened far too wide, and he howled into my face; a deafening, inhuman sound that seemed to smash aside the room. The world shifted again, violently, and suddenly I was—

I'm outside. It's early evening, with stars beginning to shine above in the deepening gloom, while the sinking sun casts lurid orange and purple across the horizon. I'm walking, my shoes scuffing against concrete as I look off to the side at the beach and the surf, waves crashing against the sand, and the low howl of the wind, and I only register the sound of footfalls behind me when something punches hard into my back, radiating ice and pain, and I suddenly can't breathe. I stagger and turn, see his face—sharp, distinctive features that stamp themselves upon my brain—and suddenly the concrete is cold against my back, I'm gasping for breath, and someone's going through my pockets, and I can't move, and I'm being dragged off the path——God, it's so dark, somebody help!—and I can hear digging and I'm being rolled over and there's sand in my eyes and in my mouth and I can't—

And then I was back in the loungeroom, kneeling in a pool of my own piss in front of an empty couch, screaming as Sarah and two policemen tried desperately to snap me out of it, while Max cowered in the corner of the room.

The cops were very kind at first. Even after I started blurting out everything. Sarah held me while the cops just nodded along as my tale became more and more insane, with Sarah interjecting to confirm the little that she'd witnessed.

Their attitude changed when I told them where Dad's body was buried.

I'd recognised the spot in that vision, you see. Hell, I'd walked past it often enough over the past four decades; a patch of sand shaded by an old bluestone wall next to the path, sheltered from wind and tides, and shrouded by a spread of littoral-loving ground cover that had gradually spread out across the top of his rough grave.

Regardless of how crazy I must have sounded, the cops clearly understood that something significant was afoot here. They took me in; not arrested, just a few questions, which became many questions, and a succession of cops asking the same questions over and over again. It took hours for someone to suggest that perhaps an investigation of the alleged grave was in order.

The body was practically mummified, nestled in a web of flaking leather and frayed polyester.

They arrested me then, of course. Their theory was that Dad had returned sometime during my adulthood, and that I'd murdered him in a fit of rage. But eventually forensics came back not only with a confirmation of identity and of murder, but of the body being over forty years old. Then came confirmation of identity, and murder. Then suspicion shifted to my mum. And when that line of questioning went nowhere, the cops—perhaps beginning to feel they were dealing with some X-Files-level bullshit—grudgingly agreed to investigate my vivid description of the killer, before hurriedly cutting me loose.

This time the media interest hasn't flagged. I've given up being polite to the journalists who come knocking. I imagine their intrusions will become unbearable once the latest developments become public knowledge.

Yesterday the police called to say that a 'person of interest' has been identified; deceased, but with belongings stowed down the back of a relative's musty garage, all but forgotten. And in the bottom of a rusted, padlocked toolbox they found a collection of old drivers' licences, one of which they want me to come and identify.

Sometimes I catch Sarah or Max looking at me. It's a very specific look:

What happened?

I have no answers; none that make sense. So we don't talk about it.

I'm not religious at all. I never used to believe in ghosts. But lately I've been thinking about amending my will to stipulate smudging or prayers or whatever's required to ensure the dead their peace. I've been given time to ensure my family never face even the slightest possibility of experiencing the trauma that I've had to deal with.

It's a gift, I suppose.

Howler

Bastards had it coming, messing with us all these years. Finally abducted the wrong guy, sucking Ted up into their flying saucer and scooting off with him, out into space, where the moon's always full.

Lycanthropy's a bitch, ain't it?

Ted tells me they tasted like chicken.

Predatory Instincts

It did not think like a human, but had learned to perfectly mimic Its prey, and so It smiled and nodded with apparent empathy as Mrs Titmangel chattered away.

"Yes, my Brian was in sales too. Always on the road, away from home. Hardly noticed when he took off ten years back—" she broke off abruptly. "Anyway, hope you haven't left *Mrs* Black at home while you're on the road, nice young man like you?"

It had only the most rudimentary understanding of human language. But the few words in her conversation It did understand, combined with a brief assessment of her tone, expression, body language and pheromones, were sufficient for It to draw an appropriate response from a vast store of memorised phrases. "No. I am not married."

She nodded happily. "Best thing really. Puts too much strain on a marriage, being a travelling salesman. S'pose you get to see the country, though, don't you? Prob'ly wouldn't even think of staying in a little guesthouse in a backwater like Hindmarsh if you weren't here on business. Will you be staying long?"

"I shall be staying for one week. May I pay in advance?" The query would secure her trust.

Mrs Titmangel beamed. "Of course, darl, whatever you like." She accepted payment, noting it in the reservations book on the front desk. "There we go. Now, I'm usually on the desk until nine p.m., but after that I'll be in my room—" she indicated a door under the staircase, "—so just knock if you need anything. Now, any bags? Just the one? Full of samples, I s'pose. My Brian had one just like it. You can carry it yourself, can't you? Big strong boy like you. I'll show you up to your room. Just you staying here at present, but I'm happy to open the dining room for you. Breakfast's at seven, dinner's at seven-thirty, although if you prefer to eat at one of the local cafes, just let me know—" and so on, all the way up two flights of stairs to room 31, where It finally took possession of the key, and—still nodding and smiling—closed and locked the door on her ceaseless prattle.

It put down the bag and regarded the darkened room. Small, dominated by an ancient wooden bedframe and lumpy mattress. Tiny ensuite. A chair. Television. Beverage-making paraphernalia. A big window, with heavy curtains tied off to the side. It stepped forward and stood for a moment, looking out over the town, lights twinkling in the dusk.

A new hunting-ground.

It carefully untied the curtains, letting them fall across the glass.

A pause.

Then, with a moist sigh, Its skin seemed to turn inside-out, clothes folding away like the wings of a cockroach. Muscles churned as ropy tentacles uncoiled. Its body collapsed in upon itself as painfully posed struts of cartilage relaxed. Human features sloughed away as It fell to the floor, adopting Its natural form. It flexed luxuriously, then scuttled under the bed, where It curled up and fell immediately into a deep yet guarded sleep.

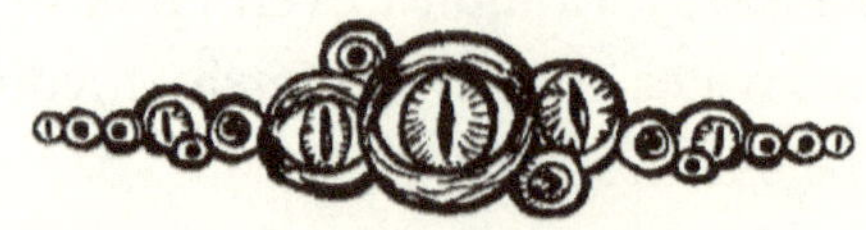

Several hours later, with the town in darkness, a black shape skittered down the side of the guesthouse, vanishing into the shadows of a neighbouring alley.

POLICEMAN MISSING! screamed the headline.

It stared impassively over the rim of Its cup at the bold print. The disappearance of the policeman would suggest the involvement of organised crime, rather than a lone salesman passing through town, but It did not wholly comprehend this. It simply knew from experience that Its actions would deflect suspicion for the duration of the feeding cycle.

"Not hungry, Mr Black?" Mrs Titmangel folded the paper away, nodding towards Its untouched plate of bacon, eggs, ham steaks, liver, kidney and black pudding.

It usually found such fare perfectly acceptable. But *cooked...*

"My apologies," It said. "I had a late dinner."

She nodded understandingly. "My Brian had a full fry–up every morning. Used to say it was the best thing after a night on the town—" she stopped, then smiled nervously. "S'posed to be terrible for you, I know. All that cholesterol. Still, young man like you should keep his strength up. Cup of tea's not enough. Nothing like a nice bit of kidney to keep up your iron, 'specially if you're running around town all day, chasing sales—"

It smiled and nodded. "Well," It said. "I expect I shall be hungry again by dinnertime."

FIVE NOW MISSING—POLICE URGE CALM!

"Knocked on your door last night," Mrs Titmangel remarked casually, nibbling a piece of toast. "Remembered your minibar was out of milk, so I knocked, but you didn't answer. S'pose you must've been asleep. Early though, only about eight–thirty, just after dark. P'raps you were out on the town."

It sensed the query behind her prattle. "I must have been asleep. I had a busy day yesterday."

"Mm. Only I *did* knock quite loudly. Not that I *wanted* to wake you, but I would've thought the noise'd wake you if you *were* in there. Just thought it was a bit odd."

It remained silent, pretending to study the newspaper.

"Well," said Mrs Titmangel, after a pause, "none of my business if you *were* out and about. Just thought it was odd 'cause you would've had to pass the front desk to go out, so I would've seen you, or at least heard you from my room, and I didn't…"

Caution. Suspicion had been aroused. But prior experience had provided It with a variety of appropriate responses. It leaned forward, favouring Mrs Titmangel with a vaguely flirtatious look. "I can assure you that I was fast asleep, Mrs Titmangel. Which is a shame. Attractive ladies do not come knocking at my door every night."

"Oh goodness!" she said, giggling. "Just the sort of thing my Brian would've said. A real ladies' man, he was. Always the charmer." Her eyes darkened. "Bit too much of a charmer, as it happens. Got him into no end of trouble. And who was it always had to bail him out…?"

It smiled and nodded, sipping Its tea.

Safe.

HINDMARSH SLASHER RETURNS TEN YEARS ON?

She had remained silent through breakfast. Unusual behaviour, which made It wary. It did not comment, merely sipped Its way through a cup of tea, then made as if to rise.

"So, where were you last night?" she asked, coldly.

It assessed her tone, stance and body–language, and opted for a polite but enquiring smile.

"You weren't in your room. Knocked on the door to say goodnight, but you didn't answer, so I thought I'd better check." Her eyes glittered. "Where were you?"

There was something almost predatory in her demeanour. *A danger, to be removed.* But to kill so close to the nest before the hunting cycle was over… It hesitated, searching for a suitably pacifying response. "Mrs Titmangel, I appreciate your concern for my welfare, but I do not feel my whereabouts last night are any of your business."

She stared back impassively. "Out at all hours, just like *him*, getting himself into trouble, bringing back his little mistakes. *Mistakes*, he calls them! My *God!* Expecting *me* to tidy up after him. *Terrible* man!" Her eyes narrowed. "I *know* what you've been up to. I imagine the police might think it was *their* business."

There was a long pause.

"I…apologise if I have upset you," It said, eventually.

She shifted slightly in her chair, waiting.

"I shall stay in tonight."

She nodded guardedly. "Well…it's a start. You do get me so upset sometimes, Brian."

It rose from the table. "I shall eat here tonight, if I may, although I shall not be back until about nine o'clock."

Her smile did not touch her eyes. "Well then, I'll prepare something special. We can eat in my room. Make it a cosy night in."

Dangerous, said her body language.

Feeding cycle ends tonight. Then move on.

It arrived back at 8.30 p.m., deliberately early, quietly closing the door behind It and setting Its bag down on the floor. The hallway was dark, the front desk unattended. The door under the stairs was slightly ajar; a thin sliver of light spilling from the gap, cutting across the floorboards. It moved to the foot of the stairs and stood for a moment, listening. No sounds of life from the upper floors. No new guests. It walked over to the door under the stairs, and knocked softly.

No reply.

Carefully pushing the door open, It entered the room beyond. Small, cosy, well–lit. Pastel prints on the walls. Two–seater couch. Thick white carpet.

Mrs Titmangel was nowhere to be seen.

It could smell her, though; feel her warmth. She had been here only moments ago.

The hunt was on.

It grinned, a thin trickle of drool leaking from a seam under Its human jaw. So much more satisfying when It had to work for Its meat. And the inevitable conclusion to this particular hunt would be especially sweet. *Annoying woman…*

It glanced around carefully. In the far corner of the room, the carpet had been folded back slightly, revealing a wooden trapdoor set into the floor—heavy, with a large brass ring attached. It stalked over, reaching out, felt the warmth increase, hooked a finger through the ring and pulled firmly. The trapdoor rose soundlessly on well–oiled hinges. A rickety ladder lead down into blackness.

It leaned forward, peering into the dark. There was nothing to fear, yet It remained cautious, not knowing the exact location of Its prey. Occasionally, prey fought back. Their teeth and nails could cause minor, if inconvenient, damage. Quickly and quietly, It descended the ladder.

Reaching the bottom, It paused, adjusting Its vision, trying to take advantage of the faint wash of light from the open trapdoor. But the light merely provided a contrast to the surrounding darkness, making it seem blacker still. It strained Its remaining senses. There was dirt beneath Its feet, and the space felt considerably bigger than the room above. Something moved slightly behind It, dry soil crunching almost imperceptibly as bodyweight shifted from one foot to the other. Flesh rubbed against fibre: fingers on a pull-cord light switch.

Beneath Its human visage, muscles flexed. Tightly-pressed membranes peeled back slightly, ready to fly open. *Wait for the light. Allow the prey to see.* Those hormones gave the meat a wonderful flavour. It grinned, anticipating the expression on her face.

"Just like my Brian," said Mrs Titmangel. "Always creeping around where he shouldn't, off with his *girls*. Coming home covered in blood, and worse. *Mistakes*, he'd say. Just *mistakes*. And always burying his damned mistakes in *my* fruit cellar. 'Til eventually I couldn't take any more. Had to send him away. But damn it, here you are again, creeping around, up to your old tricks! *Mistakes!*"

Click!

The harsh light of a single, hanging bulb spattered the interior of the cellar. Dappled the cobwebbed shelves and dust-covered jars of fruit. Spilled across the earthen floor. Pointed gleeful yellow fingers into the shadows in front of It, at the row of seven aged, decay-scented mounds of soil; at the deep, freshly dug hole at the end of the row, a shovel thrust into the pile of displaced soil beside it.

"Expecting *me* to fix things," continued Mrs Titmangel, bitterly. "Never cleaning up after himself, stupid man. Blood everywhere. May as well have left his business card at the scene. Well, I did what I could. Hid 'em away. Buried 'em. But there were too many questions, people starting to wonder, police closing in. So I had to fix that too, of course. Hide him away where they couldn't find him. Thought that'd be the end of it. But if you *will* insist upon coming back—"

She picked something up, flesh against wood. A piece of shelving? Arming herself.

Feed.

It spun around with a hiss, membranes expanding, fingers of razored gristle reaching out, jaws unhinging to bite and engulf.

She swung the axe once, the heavy blade splitting Its skull.

"And let *that* be the end of it," said Mrs Titmangel, sternly.

Where Do Horrors Come From?

About the Stories

One of the most common questions leveled at writers of all genres is: "Where do you get your ideas from?" For writers of horror, there's often the accompanying question of "Why do you write such *dark* stuff?", and occasionally, "What scares *you*?"

For me these questions are all closely related, because many of my stories are born out of personal trauma, and I find pouring that trauma into fiction to be a genuine form of therapy. It may not come as a shock, then, to hear that many of the stories in this collection are autobiographical in nature, to varying degrees; take away, say, a rampaging kaiju, or a terrifying revenant, and you're basically reading about things that actually happened to me. Other stories are a more general expression of mental anguish at specific times in my life. And sometimes the trauma at the heart of a story is derived from someone *else's* experiences; friends, family, even people I'll never meet, but whose pain affects me deeply. Empathy can be a curse sometimes, although I unreservedly encourage everyone to develop it.

What follows is an explanation of the darkness behind specific stories collected here. Be aware that, aside from the flash fiction (which gets its own collective entry), I've listed the tales in order of publication rather than the order printed in this collection, as I feel this provides a clearer, linear snapshot of the life of Chuck McKenzie, for better or worse.

So. Let's dive in. But be warned: there's much to unpack…

The Flash Fiction

I've lumped all the works of flash fiction—most totaling no more than fifty to a few hundred words—under one heading as most were born from passing fancies rather than trauma, while also being reflective of where I started as an author, twenty-five years ago. My short fiction began appearing in small press publications from 2001, mostly falling into the subgenre of humorous science fiction, and thereby securing me a reputation as a 'funny' author. My flash pieces were the purest expression of this subgenre (and perhaps more forgiving of my developing authorial skills): no room for characterisation or plot development, just a basic setup followed by a punchline. Writing good flash fiction still requires skill, but it's a very different skill set to that required for writing longer stories. I've continued to dip back into flash fiction throughout the years, as it's a great way to make use of those quirky ideas that simply don't support a longer piece. The only major development in this area is that I've mostly shifted from writing silly SF tales to writing significantly darker fare. That said, again, most of these came simply from macabre ideas that made me chuckle. The one exception is 'Daddy's Always Right', published in *AntipodeanSF* in 2023, which draws strongly upon one of my deepest personal triggers: Bad Things Happening To Kids.

Confessions of a Pod Person (2002)

This story—intended as a companion piece to the classic horror novel *The Body Snatchers* by Jack Finney—may come across as 'horror lite' to some, but I've always considered it my first proper dark tale. Firstly, it taps directly into my lifelong paranoia regarding entities that *look* human, but aren't: zombies, murderous dolls, *Doctor Who's* autons, John Carpenter's *The Thing*, and, of course, the pod people from Finney's novel. If I need to explain why this concept is so utterly terrifying, then I can only assume that you, dear reader, are one of Them.

Secondly, at the time I wrote this I was feeling very lost and alone. The Australian writing community had opened its arms to welcome me, but despite this I found myself wondering how much more I was missing out on due to my (still relatively new) responsibilities as a husband and breadwinner. My then-wife, despite being generally supportive of my writing, didn't really seem to think that what I was doing was in any way *important*, and all of this made me feel alienated from both her and the writing community. If that makes me sound like a bit of a dick, well, in hindsight, I agree. But, regardless, I was genuinely in a very poor mental state, and I didn't yet have the guidance that a diagnosis of clinical depression (which, again in hindsight, I was already suffering from) might have offered. So I (unconsciously) poured my feelings of loneliness and being an outsider into 'Confessions of a Pod Person', which—again, unrecognised by me at that point—set the standard for how I attempted to deal with personal trauma for the rest of my life.

The Mark of His Hands (2003)

As already mentioned, zombies terrify me, but I also absolutely love them (about which, more later), so writing a zombie story was something I'd long wanted to do by the time I wrote this one.

While not in any way autobiographical, this tale was certainly an exercise in dealing with some very dark personal shit. For starters, earlier that year I was diagnosed with severe diabetic retinopathy (having suffered from Type 1 diabetes since I was six), necessitating an immediate and aggressive course of laser eye surgery, with the ophthalmologist warning that there was still a very high chance of me going completely blind in both eyes. On the heels of this our first child was born, and the combination of new-parent stresses and the looming threat of blindness (plus ongoing feelings of isolation) tipped me right into a deep pit of suicidal thoughts. Being a typical guy, I didn't deign to talk to anyone about this: I just went through the motions of working, parenting, socialising and so on, wearing the fakest of smiles and thinking constantly about killing myself. Whatever you may think about the attitudes towards mental health issues and suicide today, I can tell you that both were viewed far less sympathetically back then. Depression was largely seen as something sufferers should be able to just shake off, and victims of suicide were generally seen as being supremely selfish for leaving such grief in their wake. There was virtually no social understanding of the fact that depression alters brain chemistry, often making sufferers believe absolutely that removing themselves from the world is the ultimate act of selflessness, so they won't be a burden to their loved ones. That's certainly what *I* believed. And yet, I genuinely didn't think I had an issue, as I always thought about suicide calmly and logically—not indulging in the attention-seeking wailing that I, like so many others, assumed those claiming depression tended to do. It wasn't until I read Humphrey Carpenter's biography of the legendary comedian Spike Milligan, and realised that many of Milligan's behaviours attributed to depression were exactly those I was experiencing, that I sought medical advice. My GP—upon my telling her that I wasn't *really* depressed, and the reasoning behind that belief—was utterly horrified and immediately put me on a course of strong antidepressants, opining that thinking about suicide in such cool terms was a far bigger red flag than being open and emotional about it. And while 'The Mark of His Hands' was published just prior to my diagnosis; I can see now that it reflected a great deal of the darkness in my mind at that time.

On a far more positive note, 'The Mark of His Hands' was published on the same weekend my son was born, which was the Easter weekend of that year. I still think of it as his story. And the (coincidental) timing of having a Crucifixion story published at Easter still tickles me. This was also my first story to become an award finalist—the Ditmar Award for short fiction—which I was obviously chuffed about. And yes: I *am* one of those people who genuinely thinks it's an honour just to be nominated, although, at the time of writing this, I'm perhaps unlikely to say otherwise.

Predatory Instincts (2003)

By the time this story was written and published, the antidepressants had kicked in, and I'd traded suicidal thoughts for a cold loathing of the shell I'd become. To my mind, if I had to take meds to change the way I thought then was I even *me* anymore? Much of that self-hate was channeled into this tale of a monster hiding behind a human façade, as well as obviously tapping into my long-standing fear of such entities.

As an aside, it was only when I re-read this story for the first time in twenty years while proofing this collection that I realised I'd named the entities in both 'Predatory Instincts' *and* 'The Dark Man, By Referral'—which by then I'd already chosen to be endcap stories—'Mister Black'. I'm not sure there's any significance in that, but for some reason it gave me a moment of disquiet.

'Predatory Instincts' received an Honorable Mention in *The Year's Best Fantasy & Horror Vol.17* (ed. Ellen Datlow and Terri Windling).

Retail Therapy (2004)

This was literally just a '*I fucking hate my job*' story. I was working as a salesperson in retail lighting at the time, and the customer in this tale is a composite of all the arsehole customers I'd ever had to deal with. Now, while I've mostly enjoyed working hospitality and retail over the past thirty-five years, that particular job constantly exposed me to a level of customer stupidity and entitlement I'd never experienced before (or since). The number of fellow wage-slaves who've reached out to me over the years to say they absolutely recognise the customer in this tale is depressingly large. Sometimes trauma comes from very mundane sources indeed.

Like a Bug Underfoot (2005)

In 1993 I moved from Melbourne, where I'd been working full time as a club DJ, to Sydney to fill the same role for the same nightclub chain. I loved my job, which supported both my swinging bachelor lifestyle and my functional alcoholism. One night I took home a lady I'd picked up in the club after my shift, and from there unfolded a months-long nightmare involving gaslighting, theft, fake identities, outright lies, and—eventually—the police knocking on my door and dragging her away to prison. By that time, though, I'd become fully and emotionally snared in the toxic relationship, and the shock realisation that I'd been played for an absolute idiot—together with having to face the task of repairing so many bridges with friends, colleagues and family I'd alienated due to this lady's malevolent grip on my life—drove me to my first (though not last) genuine contemplation of suicide.

Years later, when Robert Hood and Robin Pen opened submissions for their 'Daikaiju! Giant Monster Tales' anthology, I realised I had an opportunity to fictionalise that awful experience, which still lurked in my backbrain over a decade later. One reviewer wrote of it: 'McKenzie does what he does best in this story—angry, fiery black comedy with very sharp teeth. You can sympathise with the poor schmuck whose life would still be crap if his city wasn't falling around his ears'. That review was a bit of an eye-opener for me, as I'd not been fully aware of the extent to which personal trauma was saturating my fiction, and I subsequently became more self-conscious about using the darkness within as a muse, for better or worse.

Eight-Beat Bar (2005)

Having channeled a buttload of trauma into 'Like a Bug Underfoot', I balanced things out by pouring absolutely none into 'Eight-Beat Bar', which simply drew upon my experience and knowledge as a (by then) former club DJ. It was also reprinted in *Year's Best Australian Dark Fantasy & Horror 2005* (ed. Talie Helene) and was finalist for Best Horror Story at the Aurealis Awards.

The Shadow Over Bexley (2005)

I've been a fan of the writings of H. P. Lovecraft since I was about thirteen, when a like-minded classmate loaned me a tattered paperback copy of *At the Mountains of Madness*, and I simply wanted to write a Lovecraftian pastiche. However, my mental state being what it was, what I'd intended to be a light comedy piece turned a little darker somewhere along the way. Despite really liking this tale, I also think of it as my 'Cursed' story: the first market I submitted it to—a very well-respected online journal—folded weeks after accepting it for publication. So did the second publisher to accept it. It finally saw publication after being accepted a third time, although I believe that market folded soon afterwards. Clearly those Lovecraftian entities will get you any way they can.

Anyhoo. Lovecraft. Yes, the prose is often eye-wateringly purple, but Lovecraft nonetheless remains an absolute master of instilling a sense of utter dread in the reader through mere suggestion of things best left unseen. The cosmic horror subgenre that he championed and refined is, I think, one of the most terrifying concepts in horror fiction: the idea that, far from being aggressively opposed to humanity, the universe—along with the horrifying entities that occasionally cross over from the Other Side—*simply doesn't give a shit about us*. That's a real ego-popper, as well as a brutal metaphor for life in general. But then, I don't read horror in order to feel warm and fuzzy: I read it to achieve a deep and visceral sense of excitement, fear and/or revulsion, knowing full well that I can close the covers when I'm done, and head back to the mundane (though far less controllable) horrors of real life, like bills, rate rises, and interacting with (some) humans.

Of course, it's hard to mention Lovecraft nowadays without addressing his more unpleasant ideologies, which occasionally creep into his fiction. So how can I—raised a proud Leftie—still enjoy Lovecraft's work? Well, for a start, he's dead, so I'm not tacitly supporting his views by putting money in his pocket. More importantly, though, I derive genuine satisfaction in seeing the fictional universe he created constantly contributed to and built upon by authors whose very existence would have given Howard an aneurysm.

Bad Meat (2010)

Back to my love/fear relationship with zombies. I love (and fear) them in film, TV, and fiction; I love the reluctant flesh eaters of S. G. Browne's hilarious *Breathers*, the Vodou entities of Brett McBean's *The Awakening*, the heartbreaking revenants of John Ajvide Lindqvist's *Handling the Undead*, the action-packed battles against the dead in the novels of Jonathan Maberry, and the zombies featured in much of the short fiction of Robert Hood, among many others. By the by, I'm also a practicing Vodouissant (yes, really), having adopted some of the related meditative practices after researching the religion while writing 'The Mark of His Hands,' and deciding that those rituals would be useful as part of my coping strategy against depression. And it works. Having the knowledge to potentially create zombies is just a welcome extra.

Despite my obvious obsession, I've only written a handful of zombie tales myself, chiefly because I've found the process of coming up with fresh takes on the theme difficult. But for 'Bad Meat', I reached deep into my trusty pit of trauma and tapped into my horror of the scourge that is domestic violence.

Tagged (2021)

Sharp-eyed readers will note the lengthy break between 'Bad Meat' and 'Tagged'. The reason for this gap is very easy to explain: I stopped writing.

After consistently churning out fiction between 1999 and 2006, I began to find the growing pressures of family and work leaving less and less time for writing. My motivation to write was also dwindling as the antidepressants began to numb me to the darkness that had fueled my creativity. The final nail in the proverbial coffin was a lengthy article printed in a prominent Australian magazine, opining that my humorous work simply wasn't funny. Oddly, at that time I genuinely hadn't noticed that I'd become chiefly a writer of horror rather than of humorous SF, and the article infuriated me to the point where I simply walked away from it all. Absolutely stupid, in hindsight, but—despite the numbing effect of the meds—my mental health was still in a pretty fragile state, and continued to swing back and forth over the subsequent decade as I dealt with such things as the birth of a second child, several unsuccessful efforts to kick the meds, the 2010 World Science Fiction Convention being held in Melbourne (which, despite not feeling that I qualified as an author any more, I attended and really enjoyed), the end of my first marriage and the brutal divorce that followed, my kids moving away, serious health issues caused by a lifetime of diabetes and overwhelming stress from my divorce, several suicide attempts, finding a creative outlet in writing horror-related reviews for online publications, opening and managing a specialty SF, fantasy and horror bookshop, a second marriage (soon followed by a second divorce), a traumatic assault by a member of the Victorian police force (for which I later received a verbal apology), bankruptcy, the start and end of several more relationships, the pandemic, and the loss of several beloved pets, not all necessarily in that order.

And then, in late 2020, I found myself isolating at home during what became a four-month lockdown due to Covid, and—alone and staring at the same surroundings day after day after day—I began to go out of my tiny mind. Recognising that my mental health was suffering, I reluctantly decided to have a crack at writing again, hoping to fill the empty days. I looked through my ancient file of old story drafts, found one that didn't altogether suck, and began working again on the piece that eventually became 'Tagged'. At some point—more out of the need to connect with someone than from any conviction that I'd actually stick to the writing—I mentioned on social media that I was working on a new story.

Mere minutes later I received a DM from Lindy Cameron at Clan Destine Press, enthusing over my 'return to writing', and asking if I'd consider submitting something to a themed anthology she was editing. I grudgingly agreed to take a peek at the specs, with absolutely zero expectation that I'd commit to submitting anything. However, as soon as I read the specs, several individual ideas that had been knocking around in my backbrain for almost three decades miraculously fused together to form a complete story in my mind. I immediately stopped working on 'Tagged' and began working on a gonzo SF tale featuring an insubstantial talking feline—'Time Spent With a Cat'—which I submitted early in 2021. The anxiety I felt while waiting for a response was astounding. Back when I'd been churning out fiction I'd developed a decent handle on whether any given story I wrote was actually any good, but that ability had long abandoned me. So I just had to sit and wait to find out if 'Time Spent With a Cat' was irredeemable shite.

In fact, it received an enthusiastic acceptance and was published in 2022 in *Who Sleuthed It?*; an anthology of cross-genre tales in which animals assist in solving crimes.

Buoyed by the acceptance, I returned to working on 'Tagged' with significantly more enthusiasm, and it was published at the end of that same year in *Andromeda Spaceways Inflight Magazine*. It was also subsequently an Australian Shadows Awards finalist, which went a long way towards restoring my creative drive and motivation.

As to the trauma I tapped in writing 'Tagged': firstly, the city of Frankston, which I lived and worked in close proximity to for many years (on and off), and in which parts of the story take place. For those unfamiliar with the location, how shall I describe it? Well, I once got off a bus there, to be confronted by the sight of a couple of drunks crowded into the doorway of a vandalised methadone clinic, one taking a piss against the signage, the other screaming obscenities as he urged his mate to finish up before the cops arrived. And frankly, that's the best summation of Frankston I can possibly offer.

The second source of trauma is—as mentioned at the beginning of this whole shebang—Bad Things Happening To Kids (as well as my personal medical issues); clearly something that resonated with readers, as 'Tagged' became a finalist for Best Short Story at the Australian Shadows Awards.

The Dark Man, By Referral (2023)

This story explored my twin fears of domestic violence and Bad Things Happening To Kids. Regardless of the fact that perpetrators do tend to get their comeuppances in my tales (as occurs in both 'Bad Meat' and 'Tagged'), child abuse and family violence is still a pretty traumatic starting point for me, even in fiction.

Quite soon after 'Time Spent With a Cat' was accepted, but well before it saw publication, I was approached to submit a story to another Clan Destine anthology. *This Fresh Hell* (ed. Katya De Becerra and Narrelle M. Harris) was pitched as showcasing tales that took well-worn horror tropes and turned them on their heads. I immediately opted for the 'town with a dark secret' trope, as I already had a basic idea for a suitable tale (along with an opening scene that I unapologetically pinched elements of from an episode of *The Goodies*, of all things) based upon the 'Slenderman' urban legend. It took me a very short time to write it, despite the story ending up novelette length, and it was accepted immediately upon submission. I've since received plenty of very nice feedback on 'The Dark Man, By Referral' from readers and reviewers, which is lovely—especially as it's my personal favourite story as far as my entire body of work goes.

Scotoma Fatalis (2024)

Trigger warning for the squeamish: medical procedures, eye drops and related surgery.

Still with me? Okay, then.

Following my laser eye surgery back in 2003, I obviously did not go blind. The aggressive surgery did, however, knock out around forty percent of my sight (including all my peripheral vision) in order to preserve the remainder. Diabetic retinopathy being an ongoing condition, it has continued to affect me to a degree over the intervening two decades, necessitating regular check-ups with my ophthalmologist, occasional touch-up laser (and even invasive surgery), having to use eye drops daily, and limitations to my ability to travel after I voluntarily gave up my drivers' license in 2007. Despite having no peripheral vision, I could still legally have kept my license; however, I made the decision to stop driving as I couldn't have lived with myself if I'd ended up hurting someone. While all of this hasn't particularly traumatised me (aside from the original threat of possible blindness affecting my depression), I was surprised to discover that a huge number of people find the idea of applying eyedrops extremely triggering, and this eventually became one of the base elements of 'Scotoma Fatalis', along with my experience of the uncertainties that come with ongoing health issues.

The second source of inspiration for the story was a throwaway gag in Douglas Adams' *The Hitch-Hiker's Guide To The Galaxy* (which I've long considered a cosmic horror novel, as it features a powerless human protagonist cast out into an utterly wild and chaotic universe) concerning the Ravenous Bugblatter Beast of Traal, which (we are told) is so monumentally stupid that it believes if *you* can't see *it, it* can't see *you*. 'Scotoma Fatalis' is my nastier take on this idea, and—as an aside—is also one of two longer stories original to this collection.

One final note: while you might assume that the issues with my eyesight have brought me nothing but sadness and inconvenience, this is not actually the case, as I once found myself engaged in a long and intimate conversation with the objectively gorgeous dark fiction author Kim Wilkins due to her overhearing me describing to another author how it felt to receive an injection through the eyeball, and her enthusiastically jumping in to ask for further details. I call that a win.

The Gift (2024)

And finally—with this, the second original tale in this anthology—we come back to a very personal outing into trauma.

My father and mother both spent their final years battling terminal illnesses. In Dad's case it was Parkinson's, which he developed in 2010. As a younger man he'd been an athlete and an academic achiever, winning prizes for both, and kept up with both pursuits into adulthood. He enjoyed a career as a high school literature teacher, and published several related books, including one co-edited with my mum; the poetry text *The World's Contracted Thus*, which remained on the Australian syllabus for many years. He was kind and smart and artistic, and I grew up wanting to be just like him. By the time he went into care in 2018, Dad was a shell of the man I'd known my entire life—both mentally and physically—and in mid-2022 I begam writing what ended up becoming 'The Gift' as a means of coping with the loss of the person my dad had once been. I completed a full draft just weeks before he died later that same year, and couldn't find the emotional energy to keep working on it.

My mother, who shared many of Dad's passions, also forged a long career in education; first as a teacher, and later as vice principal in several well-respected girls' schools. In addition to her artistic and academic interests, she also spent her entire adult life actively engaged in supporting important social causes; she attended protests against Vietnam and the proliferation of nuclear arms, championed feminism and equal rights to all on both a personal and professional level, and even in her final years was majorly involved with the group Grandmothers For Refugees. To say I was proud of her for all this would be a staggering understatement. Just a month or so after Dad was put into care, Mum was diagnosed with mesothelioma, caused by asbestos insulation in a house the whole family had lived in when I was a child (a specter that will hang over my head for the rest of my life). Initially given just months to live, new treatments managed to hold back the cancer long enough for us to get five extra Christmases with her; time that she and I spent saying all the things that most people never think to say to one another before it's too late. For that reason alone, we both saw the cancer as something of a gift. When she eventually died on the night of Halloween 2023 I harboured no regrets over anything left unsaid, but nonetheless grieved deeply. Two days later I pulled 'The Gift' out of mothballs and added that grief to the mix.

The author Robert Hood once pointed out to me that ghost stories are, at their core, all about loss, and 'The Gift' is certainly my affirmation of that.

One final comment about this tale: when I mentioned to various people that I was writing a ghost story, the majority wanted to know if I'd ever *seen* a ghost. To me, this seems a really weird question. I mean, do crime writers get asked if they've ever murdered someone? Do authors of erotica get asked if they've personally engaged in all the acts described in their books?

Actually, don't answer that.

For what it's worth, my honest answer to the ghost question is: Yes. And I'll leave it at that. Maybe, if you ever meet me and ask nicely, I'll tell you about it. Just keep any thoughts about whether I'm crazy to yourself; I've already wondered that enough for all of us.

Endnote

These notes may make it seem like I've had a pretty awful life in many ways, but that's not the case at all. At least, not to my mind. My childhood and teen years were very happy indeed, and there have been many joyous times and events throughout the years between then and now. But as my creative muse feeds upon darkness, any explanation of the origins of my stories is always going to reference trauma rather than the fun stuff.

So, for the benefit of those who like happy endings, I can confirm that I've been blissfully happy with almost all aspects of my life over the past two years (the death of my parents aside); I have love in my life, my physical and mental health is currently as good as it can be, I've managed to successfully kick the antidepressants, I live in a wonderful city surrounded by wonderful people, and I'm currently taking a long break from full time employment in order to write, safeguard my future health, and study for a whole new career. That's a pretty damn nice position to be in.

Things may change someday. Life presents each and every one of us with constant challenges, and we deal with those challenges differently. Today I feel strong. Tomorrow I may not. But I'm determined to keep enjoying the good, and to deal effectively with the bad when it arises. That doesn't seem like a naive mission statement to me: after all, I've gone through so much already (including other traumatic experiences not addressed here, for various reasons), and I'm still not dead.

A final word on depression and mental illness in general: it's a terrible blight on society, and still—in my opinion—not talked about or supported sufficiently. And personal experience of mental health issues is so intensely subjective that even the most well-meaning advice may not be right for a given sufferer. So, if you currently struggle with mental illness, I won't offer any advice except to suggest that you speak to a mental health professional as a starting point. I will, however, quickly share a couple of personal realisations that have helped me through periods of deep and self-destructive depression:

It's better to be medicated than dead.

No matter how overwhelmingly dark life seems, things almost always get better.

Your brain is lying to you. People do care. You are not a burden.

Be as open as you can bear to be. People can't offer support if they don't know you're hurting.

And that's it. That's all I have. I hope it helps you, or someone you love.

I also hope you've enjoyed this collection, regardless of the self-indulgence of this final chapter. I have no excuse other than to say: I'm an author. A certain level of self-indulgence comes with the job.

Stay safe. Be kind. Don't be the sort of person the Dark Man would take a sinister interest in.

Chuck McKenzie
Brunswick, Victoria, Australia
February 2024

Story Acknowledgements

'The Dark Man, By Referral' © Chuck McKenzie. First published in *This Fresh Hell*, Clan Destine Press, 2023. Ed. Katya De Becerra & Narrelle M. Harris.

'The Mark of His Hands' © Chuck McKenzie. First published in *Orb Speculative Fiction* Issue 5, 2003. Ed. Sarah Endacott.

'Daddy's Always Right' © Chuck McKenzie. First published in *AntipodeanSF* Issue 292, 2023. Ed. Ion Newcombe.

'Literality' © Chuck McKenzie. First published in *AurealisXpress*, 2004.

'Like a Bug Underfoot' © Chuck McKenzie. First published in *Daikaiju! Giant Monster Tales*, Agog! Press, 2005. Ed. by Robert Hood & Robin Pen.

'Moth' © Chuck McKenzie. First published in *Antipodean SF* Issue 97, 2006. Ed. Ion Newcombe.

'Bad Meat' © Chuck McKenzie. First published in *Andromeda Spaceways Inflight Magazine* Issue 44, 2010. Ed. Felicity Dowker.

'Confessions of a Pod Person' © Chuck McKenzie. First published in *Passing Strange*, Mirrordanse Books, 2002. Ed. Bill Congreve.

'Retail Therapy' © Chuck McKenzie. First published in *Orb Speculative Fiction* Issue 6, 2004. Ed. Sarah Endacott.

Praise for Chuck McKenzie

'The Dark Man, By Referral', *This Fresh Hell*

In an irresistible blend of charm, cleverness and creeps, the boogieman used to terrify children turns out to be useful when combatting the real horrors of their lives.
Kyla Lee Ward, author of *This Attraction Now Open Till Late*

Chuck McKenzie—powerful stuff right out the gate, so well told, chilling and healing…entirely my kind of thing
Nisha-Anne D'Souza, author of *Calling Pomegranate*

This is a wonderful book for the lover of horror. I am definitely not picking favourites, but I reckon any reader will love 'The Dark Man, by Referral' by Chuck McKenzie
Clare Rhoden, author of *Dancing With Vampires Book 1*

'Like A Bug Underfoot', *Daikaiju! Giant Monster Tales*

McKenzie does what he does best in this story—angry, fiery black comedy with very sharp teeth.
Australian Speculative Fiction in Focus

Confessions of a Pod Person, **Mirrordanse Editions**

There wasn't a weak story in the entire collection, and I pretty much
devoured *Confessions of a Pod Person* in record time.
Highest recommendation on this one, kids.
Scaryminds

This collection is a valuable showcase of one journeyman author
on the rise and a worthy satirical addition to the
Australian speculative fiction landscape.
HorrorScope

Worlds Apart, **Hybrid Publishers**

I haven't been this entertained reading sci-fi since I first stumbled
across Lister and the Red Dwarf crew years back. Give it a go.
FHM

Here is a quirky, quietly humorous SF novel—with a message.
Orb Speculative Fiction

Worlds Apart is an amiable read that passed the Train Test for funny
fiction; that is, it made me laugh while reading it on public transport.
Rob Jan, 3RRR Zero-G Science Fiction, Fantasy and Historical

Worlds Apart is a fast-paced lightweight read. A lot of fun.
Aurealis

Those who are titillated by Robert Asprin's tales will find much to
amuse them in Chuck McKenzie's novel.
Altair

What the Cool Cats said about *Conversations With My Cat*

This made me laugh so loud and often, the cats left the room.
Goodreads

As a fellow cat owner (or cat servant) I needed to read this. I am so glad I did.
This book is so relatable and laugh out loud funny.
@ashisalwaysreading, bookblogger

Every cat owner (I mean cat servant) needs to read this one.
MacReady—with his witty, aloof, snarky and altogether hysterical 'typical
cat' responses to his housemate Chuck—is great. So funny.
Goodreads

Conversations With My Cat is full of dialogue very familiar to every cat
owner in the world. It's no coincidence that it's also full of the deep fondness
that humans have for their contrary and sometimes bossy best friends.
Narrelle M. Harris, author of *The Opposite of Life*

A good reminder to us of the feline persuasion of the many trials and
tribulations we face in dealing with our humans. Five purrs and two paws up.
Princess Fuzzypants, Feline Social Media Starlet

Conversations With My Cat is laugh out loud funny, and deserves all the
accolades. Get your hands or paws on this book and share it with everyone
who's ever shared their space with a cat.
Rebecca Fraser, author of *Skippy Blackfeet*

As much as I hate cats, and despise narratives in which domestic pets speak
both coherently and articulately, I found this book to be a delightful romp!
Maxwell Q. Littledog, Canine Facebook Influencer

Conversations With My Cat had me grinning from the acknowledgements
page onwards. If you are a cat person, this will prove everything you ever
imagined about cats. If you are a dog person, it will prove everything you ever
imagined about cats.
Claire Low, artist

Written in script form, which concentrates the reader's attention on the
dialogue and intensifies the humour, of which there is plenty. The
conversations are short and punchy, with plenty of LOL moments.
Edwina Harvey, author of *The Whale's Tale*